Warm Wishes,
CJ Gosling

THE
GUARDIAN

THE
GUARDIAN

SHADOWLANDS SERIES – BOOK ONE

C. J. GOSLING

Illustrations by Angela Souza

AN IMPRINT OF BRIGHTER BOOKS PUBLISHING HOUSE

Ouroboros, an Imprint of Brighter Books Publishing House
Visit our website at: www.brighterbooks.com

First Published: February, 2011

ISBN 978-0-9865555-2-7 - Trade Paperback Edition

Library and Archives Canada Cataloguing in Publication
Gosling, C. J., 1982-
The guardian / C. J. Gosling.
(Shadowlands series ; bk. 1)
ISBN 978-0-9865555-2-7 (pbk.).--ISBN 978-0-9865555-1-0 (bound)
I. Title. II. Series: Gosling, C. J., 1982- . Shadowlands
series ; bk. 1.
PS8613.O758G83 2011
jC813'.6   C2010-905796-1

Design and Illustrations © 2011 Angela Souza

Special thanks to our Assistant Editor Kelly Berthelot

Printed and bound in the USA on acid-free paper that contains no material from old-growth forests, using ink that is safe for children. One tree has been planted for this book.

for Jason

Face Your Past, Or Turn On Back...

Contents

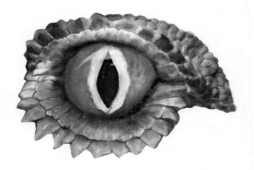

Prologue

Jin carried the fracture as an ache in his bones. The splitting of the universe stuck into his skin like glassy shards. Time passed without meaning; centuries bled from the wound, while the small creatures caught within time's flow struggled to find purpose.

Jin did not know the answer.

He sighed, jettisoning steam from his nostrils. He willed his body to become as insubstantial as mist, and he floated high through a sky darkened by the red light of a bloated and dying sun.

His destination was the South Pole, where he sensed a new threat.

He could feel the jagged shadow rend another tear into an already broken world. The rift between universes was hungry and powerful. The little ones would not know of it until it was too late.

Letting a rumble build in his belly, Jin sang his need into the wind.

His sister would hear the request and join him shortly. Together they'd stitch the tear in reality shut using their blood, singing praises to the Starbreather who lent strength to the world even still.

The air grew cold, like deathly fingers reaching up from the black frothy ocean and setting fishhooks into his flesh. Jin shuddered and called upon his Fire element to warm him. His body flared and cast tongues of flames back at the ocean. He raised his wings and swam higher through the air, closer to the pitiful heat of the dying sun.

Ahead, mountains of blue ice climbed from the ocean and built a wall towards the sky. Jin flew over the wall, tasting the edges of the atmosphere. His fire winked out, and his scales turned to starlit mirrors of ice. He folded his wings and dropped into the heart of nothingness, singing the song he'd learned at the beginning, before the universe was torn into pieces.

A man stepped forth from the shadow, the fires of Hell at his back. He touched Jin's wing as he passed, stealing from him the power of flight, infecting him with the nothingness. Jin fell crippled to the ice. He blew fire through his nostrils, his eyes reddened with pain.

The man walked where no man could walk, upon a world where humans had not been seen for centuries. Jin spurned his fear and grinned an ivory warning.

"Careful, human. I am a servant of the Starbreather. Return to your universe and I will spare your life." Jin's voice echoed to the ocean floor and split the ice. He beat a wing, calling the maelstrom. The sun fell beyond the tall ice wall and drenched them in ghostly purple. Jin sent fire into the wind and again sang the creation song.

"I do not care for your god," said the man, his reply like withered leaves. "I came here for you."

Creatures of filth crawled from dark cracks in the ice: gaping doorways leading back to Hell. They sprang upon Jin in wicked delight, unafraid of his fire or his talons. Jin roared and caught some. He tore them apart, the taste of their flesh like poison in his mouth. More came, bearing iron clubs and chains. Jin fought in desperation, longing for the freedom of the sky, yet bound by his crippled wing.

"You are the stronger one," said the man. "Your sister will be taken swiftly."

Jin trembled with rage as they pulled him down and shut his mouth with chains. The twisted creatures, their very presence an unnatural blight upon the world, jeered as they bound him.

"And once she has fallen," continued the man, "I will destroy all that you love, Elemental. This world will mourn the day they cast me out."

The man's perverse smile betrayed his madness. He struck Jin between the eyes with an iron rod and the strength of his hatred.

Jin bled and faded, remembering fear and forgetting everything else.

Magic Happens

"I will *not* go!"

Crackling bolts of blue magic tugged Aria's red hair away from her shoulders, her eyes sparking in hot rage.

"I told you, Miriam." Aria's voice trembled. Half of her fought to control the magic burning under her skin. The other half ached to let go, to show the world what a true light bender could do. "I told you I won't," she repeated. "Father can't make me."

Miriam, her lady-in-waiting, or perhaps her lady-in-keeping, licked her lips and grimly set her jaw. She pulled out the white wish rock she kept hidden among her skirts.

"My lady," Miriam edged towards her charge with a mixture of determination and sympathy. "You must be present at your brother's Initiation, and it is my job to see that you're respectable."

Aria's eyes burned with tears. She backed towards the wall and bumped against the rosewood vanity. Her hand brushed across a velvet tapestry, and she felt the weight of gold thread across its soft surface.

She loved her room. She loved everything about the palace. It had been home for as long as she could remember — and then the magic happened.

Miriam took a step closer.

"No!" Aria screamed. A blue bolt of light streaked out of Aria's pointing finger and blasted her bed. Goose down exploded upward and filled the air like falling snow. Miriam flinched, but refused to turn aside. Aria bit her lip so hard that she tasted blood. Her second bolt was better aimed. She stuck at the iron bar welded across her window. It clanged like a dropped kettle but remained in place.

Aria lowered her arm, her body trembling.

"Please," she whispered.

Miriam gathered Aria into a sticky mother-hen embrace. She clucked and stroked her hair. "There, there, love," Miriam said. "It'll all come out right in the end. You'll see." She pressed the white stone to Aria's forehead.

Aria moaned. Deep cold clawed its way greedily through

her body. It stole the heat of her magic and dropped her like a rag doll into Miriam's capable arms. Her head rolled backwards as Miriam propped her in a chair before the vanity. Aria watched the feathers from her bed drift down from the ceiling and thought that they looked not so much like snow, but like ash.

Miriam pulled the wish rock away. It shone with hard white light. Aria winced and shut her eyes. "I'm sorry, Miriam," she whispered. "I could never hurt you."

A moment later she felt Miriam begin to massage her cold fingers. "Ah, I know, love, I know." Miriam paused, clearing her throat. "It's a curse, for sure," she said. "All that magic swirling around inside of you — I get dizzy just thinking about it." Miriam patted Aria's hands.

Aria opened her eyes. She could feel warmth rising up from the wooden floor through the thin soles of her silken slippers. Gratefully she drew on the strength Mya offered her, using it to replace what the wish rock had stolen.

Miriam was all business. She knocked the feathers from Aria's rumpled gown, then pushed back her sleeves and tackled the snarls in Aria's hair. "It's that temper that does it," Miriam chided. "Just like your father. Stirs things up it does. And these fits! I swear they happen nearly every day now. Ah, but don't you worry. I heard there's talk of a cure."

Miriam's words drove the little warmth that had returned right out of Aria's blood. She sucked in a breath and coughed to hide her fear.

"It wouldn't be trouble if I had a proper teacher, Miriam." Aria said. "If Axim can do it ..."

"No more of that sort of talk!" Miriam twisted Aria's hair into heavy braids on top of her head with a jerk. "Women just aren't built for magic. We are far too emotional; as you well know."

Aria bit her tongue, her breath shallow and tight. Again the two halves of herself fought for control. She loved Miriam, but she could never explain to her what real magic was like. It moved through her veins like blood. Without it, Aria was certain she'd die.

"... It's these awful passions that ruin your complexion," Miriam prattled. "No one will want a beet-faced bride!"

The door to Aria's bedchamber swung open. Aria didn't need to look. There was only one person who dared enter without knocking.

"Is something wrong, sis? I felt some sloppy magic move through the tree. Don't tell me you've lost control again."

Axim sidled into the room like a cat fat on cream. Aria felt a rush of heat. Her eyes brightened and she forced a smile.

Miriam pulled sharply on a lock of hair. "Ah, the poor lass has a bout of the jitters," Miriam said. "There's no need for concern, young prince. She'll be ready in time."

Aria sniffed the air, imagining she could smell the decaying heart that beat in Axim's chest. Axim checked his reflection in the tall mirror by the door, carefully arranging his cape beneath the harness that held his wings in place. "Oh, I'm not worried about her. Not like she matters; not with everyone looking at me." His eyes were flat and his hands soft as a baby's. "It's just that if she doesn't make an appearance, people will wonder. They might think something was wrong." Axim's grin was pointy.

Aria thought Miriam might tear a lock of hair right out of her skull with all her tugging. Aria hardly noticed the fists she made, and she missed the thin tracings of blue sparks dancing faintly about her fingertips.

"I'm twice the light bender you are, Axim. And you know it." Aria spoke as if she were discussing what she wanted for breakfast. "Why else would father hide me away?" She leaned forward slightly. "What is everyone so afraid of?"

Axim's hands trembled — just for an instant. He turned around, his back to the mirror, and smoothed his greasy hair to his skull.

"You're a freak, sis. Girls were never supposed to have magic." Axim cocked his head. "After today I'll be a real mage, and one day I'll be king." He tried a smirk but only partially succeeded. "You should remember that."

With a smile painted on her lips, Aria snatched the hairbrush from Miriam's hand and threw it as hard as she could. Axim ducked and the brush smashed into the mirror, turning the glass into a spider web of cracked fragments.

"Freak," Axim bared his teeth and backed towards the door. "You deserve a cage."

"My lady!" Miriam gasped.

"Get out of my room," Aria said. She could feel the dark half of her sliding around in her head like a worm. Her eyes glowed with light. "You're not king yet."

Axim almost tripped on his cape as he left, his face bright purple. Aria supposed he'd tell on her to father, but she no longer cared.

"Tut, tut," Miriam said. "What an unfortunate way for a prince to act. And you, my lady — !"

Aria's mind thickened with storm clouds.

"You too, Miriam. Please leave."

"But my lady! Dinner is in an hour and the ceremony afterwards! And you in such a state!"

"Ten minutes, Miriam." Aria gripped the folds of her skirt tightly in her hands. "Just give me a little time. I'll be calmer when you return. I promise."

With a doubtful nod, Miriam backed out the door. She paused upon the threshold. "The king loves you, dear; I know that as sure as I know the sun will rise." She shut the door.

Aria heard the lock slide into place. She heard also the clink of metal as the guard beyond the door resumed his post.

Aria stood and angrily yanked a wooden trunk from the wreckage under her bed. She ran her fingers eagerly across each item within: a pair of blue shimmering wings, a spool of glossymer for repairs, and a long sharp dagger in a clever wrist sheath.

She sucked in a deep breath. It had never been a question of how, but if. Now, only hours before Axim's Initiation, she knew the answer.

Aria used the dagger to free herself of her dress and corset. She shook out Miriam's painful braids and changed into black leggings and a black, close-fitting tunic. Her wing harness fit perfectly over her new clothes. She tightened the straps into place and slid into high soft-bottomed boots.

Walking to the window, Aria took a moment to caress the soft wood about the sill. Mya, the living tree that housed and protected her family, warmed at her touch.

Aria whispered her request and the shutters upon the window burst apart as Mya flexed the walls of Aria's small chamber. The bar dropped to the floor.

Wind rushed in, playfully dousing the lamps and tugging at her wings. Loose down spun up from the floor and raced off into the night. From her window, silhouetted by dull starlight, Aria could see the dark mossy tops of the swamp trees, bending in anticipation of the coming storm.

She eased through the window and out onto a smooth branch the width of a wagon cart. She passed a few sparks into the tree, speaking a blessing of strength. She looked down. Hundreds of feet below, she could make out the colorful flickering lights of nightshift harvesting glossymer from the glowing fields at Mya's base.

"Keep them all safe, Mya," she whispered. "I'll return if I can."

Aria turned her face to the sky, her heart growing light. Most fairies refused to fly anywhere near a storm. For Aria, riding a storm was a risk she was more than willing to take. With her brother about to become a mage and her rogue female magic the worst kept secret in the kingdom, she was running out of options. Aria opened her wings and smiled with pleasure as they filled with wind.

She'd go to the place no one would dare follow.

She'd go to the humans.

The Girl In The Garden

*C*avin wiped the slick of sweat from his upper lip. He dug into his pocket, straightened the rumpled envelope and read the address in the top corner for the hundredth time.

Wanderhof Farm 6669

57613 Teilenheim Village

Germany

Part of him could hardly believe it. He'd left Berlin three days ago, sleeping on trains and brushing his teeth in public bathrooms.

The trip should have taken a day, but nobody seemed to know exactly where Teilenheim was. He'd almost given up hope that the place even existed.

Tavin's eyes lifted up from the paper, following the rutted dirt road beneath his feet to a tall black gate set in a crumbling wall. The house leaned out on the edge of what used to be a village. Emptiness poured through the broken windowpanes and collapsed roofs of the abandoned farms; green fingers of ivy climbed back in.

Tavin licked his dry lips. He supposed that for all intents and purposes Teilenheim didn't really exist at all - at least, not any more.

The rustle of barley behind him reminded Tavin that he had company.

He'd picked up his shadow on the edge of Kircheimbolanden. He could outrun anyone on the track team, but a town and two kilometers later, he still couldn't shake one annoying kid.

"What sort of idiot would go there?" the kid demanded. "What's wrong with you?"

Tavin sighed and looked the kid over. If he were anywhere else — anywhere but in the middle of nowhere with heat hitting his head like a falling sack of flour and not a bit of shade for miles — he might have wondered about the kid's clothes. His pants were too tight, his boots too tall, and he wore a purple velvet coat with girly bits of lace on the sleeves. If Tavin were anywhere else — say, a café, with a soda in his hand, talking to a pretty girl — he would have thought it odd. But here, it was just too hot to care. Tavin crumpled the envelope and stuffed it deep into his pocket. He shifted the weight of his rucksack from one shoulder to another and stepped out into the road.

"Hey! I'm telling you, so you'd better listen," the kid persisted. "That village is dead. There's nothing there."

"I thought I'd lost you," Tavin said. "Don't you have parents to bother?"

"There's no one left in that village but two crazy old people," the kid persisted. "The old lady's a witch and she forces her husband to do everything she tells him to. They'll eat you alive." The kid almost sounded excited at the idea.

Tell him. Maybe he'll leave us alone. At the light touch of his sister's thoughts upon his mind, Tavin felt his headache lessen. Their secret connection made them closer than anyone could ever understand.

Tavin squared his shoulders. "A witch might be just the thing," he told the kid. "I need some powerful magic to help me with a problem."

The kid gave him a sharp look. "You're a liar, you wouldn't dare go there."

Tavin noticed a worm dragging itself through the dust, its skinny body shiny and pink with sunburn. The house looked more appealing by the minute. The kid, on the other hand, after chasing Tavin through acres of grain in a heavy coat, didn't have a drop of sweat or a speck of dust on him.

The kid crossed his arms. "You should probably go home."

Don't. Moreanna was always bossy. Even a hundred miles away she still bossed him. *I know what you're thinking,* she said. *Remember that one-eyed cat you brought home? It ate Abigail's slipper and peed on your math homework.*

Tavin rolled his eyes mentally.

"Look," he said to the kid, "that house is the only place around with water and shelter. I don't know why you followed me here, but if you promise to keep quiet, I'll let you come the rest of the way."

"You — you want me to come with you? That place is haunted!"

Tavin wasn't listening; instead, he bent down to examine the worm. He wondered if a worm could get sunburn or if he just thought it could.

"No way," the kid replied. "You really are crazy!"

Tavin shrugged, trying to pretend he felt better about the whole thing than he actually did. He scooped the earthworm into his palm and dropped him into his pocket with a handful of dirt for good measure. "It'll be fine."

"What makes you so sure?"

"They're my grandparents." Tavin said.

The kid yelped. Tavin, a wry grin on his lips, heard him dash back towards the barley stalks. By the time he straightened up, the kid was already gone.

Oma Nadia stirred her tea counter clockwise and inspected Tavin over the top of wire-rimmed glasses. Her fingers were thin and her free hand twitched unconsciously over the placemat.

"How old are you?" she asked.

"I'm getting close to sixteen," he said.

"You're fifteen," she corrected.

A large round clock counted down the seconds with precise clicks. Tavin sat with his grandparents around a small table that reminded him of a school desk he used to have — the one where his long legs knocked against the bottom.

Opa winked. "What a clever, handsome boy he is, Nadia. So much like Julias, just like a movie star."

Tavin tugged self-consciously on the rumpled band shirt he wore. Neither the dark color nor bright neon graphics could hide the dirt stains he'd collected sleeping in the same shirt for three days. He hardly felt like a celebrity.

Oma sniffed. "You'll ruin him, Klause. A child should never know he is handsome. Work is more important."

"Ahh," Opa tapped his nose. "Alas, I should have married a horse."

Oma rapped Opa's knuckles smartly with her spoon. Opa made a face and wriggled his eyebrows at Tavin.

Tavin snorted. His father had always said his grandparents were dangerous, but now that he saw them, Oma and Opa appeared about as threatening as fruit flies. He pulled the creased envelope from his pocket and placed it in the middle of the table. "Dad tried to hide these from us but some of your letters got through anyways. Morry kept them all. She gave me this letter to help me find you."

Oma didn't even bother to look at the letter. "What have you been telling the children, Klause?" she asked. "What nonsense did you write now?"

"Only chickens and cows and rain," Tavin said. "Morry likes them."

Opa rubbed his hands together. "Finally, we have a chance to get to know our grandson. What a wonderful thing! I will write your sister some more. She should also come."

"She can't travel," Tavin replied. "She's sick."

Opa's face softened. Oma continued stirring her tea, her expression granite.

"Tavin," Opa said. "We know it has been hard. You must understand, when your mother died we wanted to come. We wanted to take care of you and Moreanna. But Julias — "

"I know," Tavin said. He flicked his bangs out of his eyes and pulled his elbows in. "Dad made you stay away. He said that all the things you told us as kids — the stories of magic — were lies. When he left he paid our housekeeper to watch out for us rather than send us here."

"Then why have you come?" Oma said. "Surely your father would not approve."

Tavin shifted in his chair, hardly able to believe what he was about to ask. He supposed his grandparents fit the profile. He wondered if they'd ever even seen a computer. Still, despite the old farmhouse and Tavin's special connection to his sister, he had a hard time imagining his grandparents stirring potions and chanting spells.

"Morry's not just sick," he said. He dug into his pocket and began fiddling with the rubber band he found there. "I mean, whatever she's got it's nothing the doctors can figure out. They don't know what's happening. She's just — fading away." Beneath the table, Tavin's hand tightened into a fist.

"Tavin ..." Opa reached out a clawed hand and let it drop on Tavin's shoulder. Tavin tried not to flinch. He hated it when people pitied him. He reached for a piece of cake for an excuse to shrug off his grandfather's hand.

"I am sorry about Moreanna," Oma said. "But I don't understand; what do you think we can do?"

Tavin chewed slowly. "The stories" he said, "all those stories about magic you told us about before dad told you to stop visiting — Moreanna doesn't think you just made them up. She thinks you can help."

"Hmmm." Oma took a sip of tea. Tavin forced himself to release the breath he'd been holding. There, he'd said it.

"And how are you?" Opa asked. "Have you been ill as well?"

A dull headache pounded against his temples. "I'm fine," he lied.

"You have grown very much," Oma said. "I am sad to hear my son has abandoned his children. He left us also, when he refused to become a farmer like Klause and moved to the city."

Opa gave Oma a sharp look but said nothing. Oma watched Tavin with a steady and closed expression. "Please understand," she said at last. "These last years have not happened as we would have wanted. You are welcome to stay in our home. If you wish it, we will send for your sister and help the best we can. But you must not put hope in children stories; there is no magic here."

Opa continued to stare hard at Oma. For a moment Tavin thought he would speak, but instead his grandfather simply poured himself a second cup of tea. The intensity of Tavin's headache increased. A dull fiery ache stirred deep in his belly.

Tavin pushed his chair back abruptly, knocking a saucer to the floor. It fell and shattered with a loud crash that startled Opa out of some far-away daydream. Oma's spectacles flashed.

"Come." Opa jumped diplomatically between Tavin and the broken dish, ushering Tavin towards the door. "Have no worry about such a small little thing. My Nadia can clean it easily. I am sure you want to rest after your long journey." Opa glanced over his shoulder. Oma, fetching a broom from the corner, had her back to them both.

Tavin felt his anger calm beneath Opa's cool touch. "Sure," he said. "I think I'll stick around for a bit. I think it's time we really got to know each other."

Opa grinned and wiggled his eyebrows. "Wonderful! I have the perfect room for you."

That night, the moon rose large as a dinner plate. An odd yellowish color, it struggled as it climbed, like a gull fat from his greedy dinner.

So, what news?

Moreanna's voice was faint. She had to ask three times before Tavin noticed it. Tavin rubbed his head, feeling as if someone were beating his skull with a rubber mallet.

They're liars. I don't know what it is, but they're hiding something. Tavin sat on the edge of his bed and watched the night deepen through the open balcony door. His bedroom was small with thick plaster walls and wooden floorboards. A tall wardrobe leaned in one corner, a bookcase in the other. The balcony had black iron rails and overlooked a lush and mostly wild garden. The room itself was nestled on the end of a long hallway. It was so far away from the main part of the farmhouse that it felt like a different country.

Tavin, Moreanna said. *Calm down, you'll feel better. You never did deal with your anger well.*

Tavin kicked at the rucksack at his feet. Moreanna loved psychology. What made it worse was that she was right. He took a few deep breaths, closing his eyes until he felt his heartbeat slow down.

The blankets on his bed remained untouched. He still wore a dusty pair of high-tops and his army jacket. In his right hand, he played with the rubber band he always kept in his pocket: stretching it, weaving it, and snapping the rubber band urgently between his fingers. With his left hand, he opened the small plastic bottle he carried in his duffle and swallowed a couple of painkillers.

Tavin sighed. The soft scuttling noise of tiny feet caused him to look down. A rat with a tattered ear, its scraggly body so thin Tavin could see its ribs, darted out from under the bed. Glad to know he had company, Tavin lifted his feet to clear the way. The rat vanished behind the bookshelf.

Morry?

He'd lost the feel of her thoughts inside his head. He flipped open his cell; no reception of course. It was disconcerting not to feel her there. It felt like a part of him was missing. He fought the urge to try to reconnect mentally. He needed her to stay strong.

Tavin unzipped his duffle and opened a package of stale cookies. He crumbled one between his palms and dropped to his belly.

"Here, little guy" he coaxed. "Don't worry, I'm all alone. I won't hurt you."

The corner where the bookshelf leaned was grimy with dirt and cobwebs. A small passage, just big enough for him to fit his hand into, opened behind the bookshelf at the bottom of the wall.

Tavin pushed the bookshelf back and squirmed forward. "Something sweet for you, ratty." The very tips of his fingers passed into the darkness. Tavin gritted his teeth, preparing to be bit for his troubles. He felt the soft brush of whiskers against the back of his hand. He held his breath, forcing himself to stay still. Clever little fingers grasped at the cookie pieces. Tavin smiled. Moving slowly, so as not to alarm his new friend, Tavin backed away from the wall and up onto his knees.

"You sure are a strange kid."

Tavin yelped in surprise and knocked his head against the bedpost. The kid from the road stood in the corner of his room: velvet coat, widow's peak, pointy chin, and black eyes as cold as outer space.

Told you. Moreanna was back. *I told you not to encourage him. You get into all sorts of trouble every time you bring things home.*

This time Tavin was inclined to agree. He climbed to his feet with a nervous laugh. "Okay" he said, "you got me. People usually can't sneak up on me like that." Tavin crossed his arms using his grown-up face. "You're going to have to tell me who your parents are. I know this place looks run down but people actually do live here. You have to leave."

The kid straightened a sleeve with a tug on the lacy cuff. He strolled towards Tavin and thrust out a gloved hand. "My name's Demetre," he said.

Out of habit, Tavin reached forward. His fingers passed through the kid as if he were nothing but a chilly breeze. Tavin snatched his hand back, feeling deep cold spread up his arm. He would have yelled again, but the kid swiped a ghostly hand across Tavin's throat, freezing his cry before it could begin.

"Told you this place was haunted," Demetre said. He snickered.

Tavin collapsed upon the bed, rubbing his throat. "What are you?" His heart felt like it would pound right through his chest.

"I used to be like you," Demetre said. He watched Tavin with a gaze too old for his childish face. "I had questions and I came here for answers. This is what happened." Demetre shrugged. "Sorry about the cold. It'll pass soon. The handshake was a joke, but I couldn't let you yell again. If your grandparents find out about me, I'm finished."

Tavin's eyes measured the distance to the door — too far. The balcony was closer.

He struggled to move but Demetre's ghostly touch made his legs and arms sluggish. "Were you murdered?" he asked.

Demetre grimaced, his body colorless in the moonlight. "It would have been better if I was. No, the ones who did this to me trapped me in a place between this world and death. I've been trying to find a way back ever since." Demetre shrugged. "So far, this is the result."

Tavin shuddered as the last of the cold touch left his body. He coiled his body like a spring, ready to make a dash for it.

Demetre glided towards the balcony, leaving a clear path to the door.

"Run if you want," he said. "I only want to help."

Do it, Moreanna urged. *Get out of there, Tavin.* She'd begun to fade again.

Tavin sprang to his feet, mentally mapping the quickest route through the sprawling house and outside. His hand closed about the doorknob.

He hesitated. "Was it my grandparents?"

Demetre shook his head. "No, but I wouldn't trust them if I were you."

Tavin turned the knob.

A slight smile formed on Demetre's lips. "I know what happened to your father."

Tavin froze. His heart all but stopped. He wanted to go, but his legs refused to move.

"He went to look for your mother," Demetre said.

"She's dead." Tavin's mouth was dry.

Demetre shrugged. "Death isn't always simple."

Tavin clenched the doorknob, his palm sweaty. "That's impossible. I saw her die. My father left because he couldn't handle the grief.

He didn't go looking for her, he went mad!" Tavin shouted the last sentence. His fear forgotten, he swung around to face Demetre, fire in his belly, his face hot.

"I promise, as long as you stay quiet, I won't touch you again." Demetre cocked his head. "Use your gift. Everything I'm telling you is the truth."

"What do you mean, 'my gift?'"

"I told you, I'm like you." Demetre took a step forward. "I know about the headaches, how you can see through lies like tissue paper in the sun. You read people." Demetre leaned forward, "You're different; we both know it."

Tavin frowned. "How can I be sure you're not just leading me on?" he said.

Demetre arched his eyebrows. "You can't be."

Tavin surrendered. He walked away from the door and sat down on the bed. He dropped his head into his hands. "Tell me what you know."

Demetre smiled. He pointed through the glass balcony door and towards the garden below.

"What do you see?"

With heavy steps, Tavin crossed the room and walked out onto the balcony. Demetre followed, close on his heels. A leafy tree crowded against the balcony railing. Awash in moonlight, the verdant garden looked like a black and white photograph, the shadows sharp enough to cut.

"The door," Demetre pressed. "There, behind the tree."

Tavin stared hard at it. It looked like a normal door: made of wood with a black latch, but something told him differently.

"It's a Gate," Demetre whispered. "Two years ago I saw your father walk through."

"Where does it go?"

Demetre looked hard at him. "Someplace else," he said. "A place that looks like our world but is not meant for humans."

Something shifted in the garden below.

"What's that?" Tavin felt the movement of cold air against his cheek. He turned in time to see Demetre flee back into the room.

"An enemy," he hissed. "I can't be seen. They'll send me back."

Tavin shifted into the shadows, curious to see what could frighten a ghost.

A slender silhouette straightened up from a bed of wildflowers.

"It's a girl," he said in surprise.

The girl slid a knife into her belt and held a bloom up to the moonlight. She gently cradled the roots in one hand, her lips curving into a smile. She moved like an animal, her dark hair glinting red and sliding over her shoulders like silk.

Demetre began to fade. "Let this be your first lesson," he said. He thrust out a finger. "That - that *creature* is nothing but trouble."

Tavin blew out his cheeks and raised his hand to gnaw on a fingernail. "They always are."

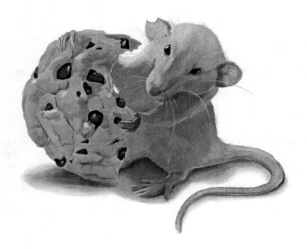

The Thirteenth Mage

Tavin climbed over the balcony rail and jumped. His sweaty hands caught a branch and slipped off. He would have fallen right there, but he somehow snagged another branch with his arm and leg. He hung for a moment, catching his breath.

A pale hand snaked out of the darkness and grabbed his ankle, giving it a sharp tug.

Tavin tightened his grip, but the branch cracked and he tumbled to the ground.

"Ow!" Tavin rubbed his head and tried to rise, freezing at the touch of a knife pressed against his chest.

Something dangerous lurked behind the girl's luminescent green eyes.

Despite the knife she held, a hot thrill passed through Tavin. He lay still, fixing on what he hoped was his most charming smile.

"Easy," Tavin said, "I didn't mean to sneak up on you. There's no need for that."

Her gaze narrowed cleverly. She began to speak in a rolling tongue that Tavin didn't recognize. She pointed at him and then at the tree. She laughed.

"It's not funny," Tavin's cheeks grew hot. "Pulling people out of trees is not a good way to make friends."

She looked at him sharply. Tavin didn't realize he was pouting until she jabbed a finger at his bottom lip, mimicking his face.

The knife wavered and Tavin saw his chance. He jumped forward, throwing her onto her back and pinning her with his knees. He yanked the knife away and threw it into a clump of long weeds.

"Sorry," he said. "I don't like knives around my throat." Tavin shook his bangs away from his eyes, unable to stop staring. She was the most beautiful girl he'd ever seen. Her skin shimmered in the moonlight. Her green eyes actually seemed to glow. She even smelt wonderful — like warm blackberries and autumn apples.

The girl growled and kneed him in the stomach. He crumpled forward with a gasp. She yanked hard upon his arm and leveraged him through the air with her feet. Tavin fell with a grunt against the garden wall, not far from the wooden gate.

Tavin staggered to a stand in numb surprise. He must be twice her weight, yet she'd thrown him with ease. The girl ran towards him and snapped a kick at his ribs. He caught her foot in the crook of his arm and pulled. For one glorious moment, she fell into his arms. Her intoxicating scent washed over him. He drew her closer, and she head-butted him in the chin, smashing his skull against the garden wall.

With fireworks shooting across his vision, Tavin released the girl and stumbled backwards. He fell ungracefully on his rump. He reached for the wall and crawled clumsily back to his feet.

The girl watched him closely, her hands on her hips. Her eyes glowed bright green.

"Stupid human," she said. "Now the keeper is awake."

"Wait — ," Tavin shook his head, trying to clear away the static that buzzed through his brain. "You can speak my language? Who are you?" He looked up.

The girl was gone.

Tavin leaned against the wall with a groan. He wasn't sure what hurt more, his head or his pride. He'd just been beat-up by a ninety-pound girl. A loose grin tugged on his lips. He just had to know her name.

Tavin felt the garden gate grow hot beneath his palm. He yelped and pulled his hand back in alarm. The edges of the gate crackled with blue light and the wood began to glow. He hastily stumbled back.

The shadows grew darker and the air thickened. Cold wind

spun through the garden, tearing at the flowers. At the center of the whirlwind, the darkness gathered together and turned solid, forming into the rough shape of something like a large pro-wrestler: its head was square and its eyes toxic green.

His heart beating like a cavalry charge, Tavin bolted around the thing towards the balcony. He leapt and caught hold of the lower rails.

The monster lumbered towards Tavin with fists like cannonballs. Tavin swung his body and hooked a leg over the lip of the balcony. He glanced over his shoulder to see the monster raise a shadowy hand. Tavin pulled himself higher. If he could just get to the house —

A bolt of green light shot out from the monster's arm, striking Tavin from behind like ten thousand electric volts. Tavin's hold on the balcony slipped. He was unconscious before he hit the ground.

The wind rushed coldly through the barley beyond the garden wall. The gangly figure turned up the collar of his rain slicker and pulled the brim of his wide floppy hat low over his eyes. He glanced over his shoulder once then moved resolutely forward, following a winding track through the waving grain.

He'd left the boy alive, and sent the garden golem back to the shadows — which was more than the others would do if they ever caught the boy opening a Gate. The creatures of the Shadowlands made no distinction between accidental trespassing and invasion.

All the more reason for peace.

The man walked deep into the night, counting his steps. At last, he came to a dimple in the ground between fields, covered by a dense thicket. He hesitated then pressed his palm against the trunk of a gnarly apple tree. The thicket in front of him glowed with blue light and untangled. The thorns, briars, and branches drew apart to form a narrow door.

The man squared his shoulders and stepped forward through the Gate. His ears buzzed and his gut felt like someone had tied it into knots. The night grew darker.

The first thing he always noticed was the smell. The air hung damp and heavy, carrying with it a sweet sickly smell like a cross between rot and congealed blood.

Swamp water oozed against his heels. The small thicket now towered above him with long sharp thorns. The twisted apple trees bent together like the columns of a crumbling cathedral.

The man hurried forward down the winding path between the trees, knowing that what lay ahead remained free of the horrible stench of decay. Soon he came to a break in the tangled thicket. A clearing, covered in short silver grass and lined by silver-barked beech trees opened before him. The man stopped, enjoying the taste of clean air again.

At the centre of the clearing, a round pool pulsed light with the rhythm of a heartbeat. Not a ripple touched the pool's surface, yet it was alive with swirling pearly colors. The magical pool cast colored light that illuminated the roof of tangled branches overhead.

Creatures slid from the shadows of the thicket and towards the light of the pool. Some almost looked human. One creature lurched forward, stiffly erect and wearing a military uniform. Then the shadows changed and revealed evil yellow eyes and sickly spotted gray skin. A long string of drool dangled from the goblin's large bottom lip as it glared at the man with brutish resentment.

Encircling the gathering, its vaporous body weaving around and through the trees, was an Elemental. Her gigantic lion-like head rested serenely on the grass near the pool. She studied the man with a steady unfathomable gaze.

A willowy tree sprite stepped out of her tree. She sidled near to the man, her wine red hair floating straight up from her head. Her slender fingers wandered playfully across the man's chest.

"You enter this place at the cost of your life, human," she said. "Don't tell me you weren't warned."

The man set his feet firmly into the ground. "I have a right to be here. The council isn't complete without its thirteenth mage."

A muscular, nearly naked gargoyle smiled unpleasantly. Crude tattoos covered the gargoyle's stony hide. It wore a heavy broad sword strapped to its back between large bat-like wings. "A rune for each kill," the gargoyle said. "And I've still got room for you!" Rude laugher erupted from the other creatures. With a rush of wind and the parachute snap of wings, the gargoyle rocketed forward.

The man raised his right hand and several large glowing green stones erupted from the earth, striking the gargoyle in mid leap. The beast tumbled over in surprised pain.

Abrupt silence fell around the pool. All eyes were fixed upon the large white scar in the shape of a star on the man's open palm. Resentment and fear brewed together, thickening into hatred.

The goblin spat. "Human magic!" it said. "You can't kill us all."

The tree sprite draped her pale arms over the man's shoulders. "How about a kiss, love," she whispered. "One kiss and you won't feel it when they take your skin."

"Enough!" A stag with pure white flanks, black eyes, and a wide crown of antlers walked into the light cast by the pool. He was larger than a horse and his voice sounded like a deep ringing bell.

"Lord Ieda!" The man took off his hat and bowed. He was bald except for a few wild wisps of gray hair above his ears. "I didn't expect you to be here."

"And why not?" asked the stag. "Am I not the Emperor? Can I not go where I please?" The Emperor began to glow with light. His form wavered and changed, flowing together. When the light faded, he'd transformed into an old man with black eyes and a white beard that hung nearly to his feet. He wore a gray robe and a thin silver circlet sat upon his head.

The trees behind him bent themselves down into a throne for the Emperor to sit on.

"The human is correct," the Emperor said. "The thirteenth mage still has a right to speak at this council. He will not be harmed."

The creatures stirred unhappily about the pool. The tree sprite hissed into the man's ear before stepping back into her tree. The man knew how close to death he'd been. He clasped his hands together to steady the shaking and cleared his throat.

"My brothers and sisters, as you must know, there are more Gateways between our worlds than ever; there are too few of us left to guard them." The man's accent was thick and slow, yet he spoke his simple words with care. "The lines are blurring; the borders are not as sure as they once were."

"We shall double security!" The goblin said. "And make an example of trespassers!"

The man shook his head. "I have a greater concern. I suspect that other borders may also be growing thin. I have already seen the dead begin to walk. Their world is not so far away from ours." The man hesitated. "I am worried about Golgotha," he said.

"The hell world?" The Emperor frowned. "No one returns from there, dead or not."

"Maybe," the man said. "But how can we know for sure? If that ancient barrier were to break, it would unleash a tide of enemies upon both our worlds, bent upon total destruction. I believe the first among those to return would be the Unmaker."

Shocked silence greeted the man's words.

The gargoyle broke the silence with a guttural growl. "Never," he said. "It's impossible."

"With the barrier between Golgotha and our worlds growing weaker, it's something we must consider." The man squared his shoulders and tightened his jaw. "We should prepare."

"Even if this is true," the Emperor said, "it would take immense power for him to regain his former strength. There are very few of us who wield that power. And none would help him."

"I am not so sure of that, he had supporters once." The man stared into the faces of the gathered creatures as if mining their souls. "We both know he will strike your world first," he added softly.

"Liar!" The tree-sprite's eyes fluttered wide. "It's a human trick!" The man shook his head, opening his palms.

"You are all in danger, and you need help. If you open your borders to us, as you did in the old days …" the man paused, measuring his words,"… we would be willing to fight at your side."

A roar rose from the assembly. The magical creatures jeered, hurling insults. The gargoyle snarled and brandished his sword. "We'll never trust a human! You're a fool! Go back to your world. Tell whatever is left of your kind that if they dare to cross into our world they will be killed!"

The man refused to flinch. He looked around the clearing, meeting the eyes of all he could. "I've done my duty and warned you," he said. "Your blood will be on your own head. But do not fear; if you should call on us for aid, brothers, we will be there."

The man walked back up the path with the rustle and crackle of thorny vines at his heels, the creatures jeering at his back. Only two remained silent.

The Emperor's dark eyes lingered upon the spot where the human mage had stood, his thoughts returning to an ancient time when humans and magical creatures fought together to preserve their worlds from evil.

The other creature to stay silent was the Elemental. With eyes swirling with ancient and hidden wisdom, the Elemental looked into the future and pondered what she saw.

"What a nasty fall you had. You're lucky Opa found you." Oma looked sternly at Tavin over the top of her glasses. She sat closely by his bed, knitting a sweater in black and purple. "Boys your age should know better than to go jumping about like they are crazy, climbing old trees at night."

Tavin sat up, his head in his hands. The light through the balcony door was the orange color of late afternoon. He'd nearly slept through the day.

"No." Tavin's tongue felt thick. "There was something else." It felt like a dream. He struggled to remember. "I saw a girl," he said finally. "There was a girl in the garden."

"There was no girl." Oma didn't even bother to look up. "Opa found only you."

"She was about my age; short, with dark red hair."

Oma shrugged. "All the children have moved away to the cities. They do not care if we must sell our farms when we are too old to work them."

Tavin shook his head. "This wasn't a dream." He hesitated, suddenly unsure. The girl was one thing; the monster was another. All at once, he wasn't sure if he wanted it to be real or not.

Oma's knitting needles clacked. "You are too young to have a girlfriend. And what if her family does not approve? When I wished to marry Klause I had to first study at a farmer's school to learn to be a good farmer's wife. Will this girl do such a thing? Or is she simply a rebel?" Balls of yarn rolled around on the floor like a tangled spider web.

Tavin's cheeks burned. "Not that it's your business but I've had girlfriends before, and if two people love each other who cares about what our families think?"

Oma clicked her tongue. "A girl who is a rebel does not make a good wife and a boy who gives his heart so easily is foolish."

Tavin jerked his covers back. "Whatever." He began to stand and froze as he realized he was bare from the waist up. He sucked in a quick angry breath.

"What did you do with my shirt?"

Oma Nadia peered at him over the top of her spectacles, arching her eyebrows at the chilly note in his voice. "Do you sleep with your clothes on? This is not a good thing. You will get my nice clean sheets dirty."

"You don't just pull off a guy's shirt!" Tavin flushed with humiliation, wrapping his arms around the large ragged scar that cut its way across his chest. He hated the look of it in the mirror; he hated the look on people's faces more. He didn't even let his sister see him this way. Fury turned his face bright red. "You had no right!"

Oma looked at him thoughtfully. "Does your head hurt?" she asked. "You should drink your tea." She pointed to a brown mug on his nightstand. A thick steamy liquid gurgled inside. It smelled like pickled cabbage. Oma turned back to her knitting. "Your clothes are clean and in the wardrobe."

"Are you blind?" Tavin's voice shook. He jabbed a finger towards his chest. "You've seen me now; you might as well get an eyeful. Just don't you dare pity me."

Oma's eyes crinkled. She might have been smiling. "What does an old wrinkled lady like me have to do with someone so young and handsome? My Klause keeps me warm at night; I need not look."

"Oh, gross!" Tavin made a face and dove for the wardrobe. "Please, don't ever say that to me again. And don't think you can give me advice about girls either. And please, please leave now. I want to get dressed."

"Ach vey! If you wish it." Oma hobbled towards the door, her eyes laughing. "You should not always be so upset," she said. "It will make your stomach ache. You must rest. Drink your tea and sleep. When you wake up I'll have some more plum cake waiting in the kitchen for you."

Tavin stared after Oma in disbelief as she left, still raw from his humiliation. "Plum cake? Plum cake!" he muttered. "That old witch!" Tavin grabbed the mug and stalked out onto the balcony, dumping the noxious potion into the garden. He could almost see the flowers begin to wither. A hard lump formed in his throat and his hand wandered up to his chest.

I miss mom too. Moreanna fed him what comfort she could.

Tavin pushed her angrily away. *I don't want to talk about it.*

An inquiring squeak came from under his bed. A moment later the skinny grey rat with one chewed ear brushed past his legs.

"Oh, go back to bed, you little pip squeak," Tavin told the rat. "I'm fine."

Tavin clenched the railing hard enough to turn his knuckles white. The scar on his chest left a hole in more ways than one. His eyes felt dry and itchy. He rubbed them irritably; he'd stopped crying about it years ago.

The rat remained where it was, trembling and watching Tavin with expectant eyes. With a shake of his head, Tavin returned to his duffle and fished out the cookie bag.

"You must be hungrier than I thought." Tavin laid his palm with the cookie chunks open upon the floor. The rat bolted under the bed but returned a moment later, circling nervously in front of Tavin's hand.

"I know what you're thinking," Tavin said. "You've seen it before. You think it's a trap." Tavin dropped a few crumbs on the floor and drew back. These the rat eagerly gathered, stuffing its cheeks greedily.

"Well, I'm not like the others," Tavin said. "I'm not going to hurt you." He placed a big chocolaty chunk in the center of his palm, and dropped his hand back to the floor. This time the rat grew bold enough to inch onto Tavin's open hand. When Tavin didn't move, it bit into a corner of the cookie and began dragging it back. Tavin couldn't help the small smile that crept its way onto his lips.

Bit by bit, Tavin brought a finger down onto the rat's soft grey coat. The creature stiffened, but didn't run.

Tavin slowly stroked the rat's back. "Well," he mused. "Don't we make a pretty pair; a burn victim and a starving rat."

The rat squirmed out from beneath Tavin's fingers and continued dragging its treasure towards the bed.

"Pip squeak ..." Tavin scratched his cheek. "That's not a bad name. If we're going to be roommates, I'll have to call you something. How about Pip?"

Pip was back. Having safely stowed his cookie chunk he began exploring the open duffle bag for more food. Tavin laughed and picked him up. The rat squirmed a little but didn't seem inclined to bite.

"Not so fast, Pip," Tavin said. "It's not good to eat it all at once." He put the rat on his shoulder and began rummaging for his jacket. He found it, pressed and neatly hung in the wardrobe. Tavin narrowed his eyes. Who ironed jackets? Only old people bothered with that sort of thing.

Tavin placed Pip on his nightstand while he dressed, then picked him back up. He made a face. Pip had already left two rice-sized droppings behind. Tavin sighed and used a dirty sock to knock the droppings into the wastebasket. He paused, looking back out through the glass balcony door. His thoughts returned to last night.

Had it really been a dream? He found it hard to believe. Monsters or not, if Oma wouldn't tell him he'd have to find the truth out on his own.

"I wouldn't if I were you." Demetre appeared out of thin air, sulking out from the shadows above Tavin's bed. He settled himself on Tavin's headboard and made a face. "Do you always talk to rats?"

Tavin crossed his arms. After his experience in the garden, a ghost no longer frightened him. "He's prettier than you. What do you want?"

Demetre floated towards the floor. "I told you that girl was trouble. If you'd listened to me, you might have avoided waking up the golem. It's his job to guard the Gate. Now you've put him on high alert. You'll have to go another way."

"What are you talking about?"

"I'm talking about crossing over of course. I mean, that's why you're here, isn't it?" Demetre tilted his head to the side. "There's magic in the Shadowlands. Maybe you can find something to help you with that problem you've got."

Tavin fell silent as he absorbed this information. His stomach bunched in knots and his mouth went dry. "It wasn't a dream."

"Of course not. You know it wasn't. You can feel it." Demetre's eyes gleamed. "Last night you woke up a shadow golem. Some time ago, someone powerful took a pebble and stretched its shadow into the shape of a monster. The creature then took on the powers of whoever created it. It's tricky magic. Golems aren't real, which makes them hard to kill. If they have you long enough, they'll turn you into a shadow as well. The really nasty ones like to pull your skin — ," Demetre laughed at the expression of horror on Tavin's face.

"Morry was right about this place." Tavin's stomach remained clenched so tight it began to ache.

"Now you get it," Demetre said. "You're going to need help

getting there."

Tavin kneeled to the ground, his head spinning. He forced himself to take a few deep breaths.

"What's the matter?" Demetre asked. "You're not afraid, are you?"

Of course he was. He'd do anything for his sister, and the thought of where that might lead terrified him. He pulled a knife out of his duffel and slipped it into his pocket. "No golems," he said. He spoke the words carefully, working to stop them from quavering as he spoke. "You know a way?"

Demetre's smile froze. "There's a hidden door," he said. "One they've forgotten about."

Tavin steadied his hands and laced up his sneakers. He wished he hadn't pushed Moreanna away earlier. He needed to feel her now, but when he reached for her all he felt was cold emptiness. Deep down Tavin felt a hot spark of anger stir at the thought of Moreanna's sickness. He felt another flare of anger at the fact that he had to search for a cure alone. His father should be the one to face monsters, not him. Tavin stood, his teeth on edge, the last tatters of his childhood falling away from him like a torn cloak.

"I'm ready."

"This way." Demetre glided out of the bedroom and down the hallway. Tavin followed. The smell of fresh plum caked wafted faintly down the corridor from the direction of the kitchen, enticing and infuriating Tavin at the same time.

Demetre turned a corner and dropped down a wide stairwell that wound its way towards the main foyer. Squinting in the dim light, Tavin felt his way down the stairs. Demetre, glimmering like a beacon, waited for him halfway between the two floors. He pointed a hand towards a discolored section of the wall.

"There," Demetre said. "You'll have to figure the rest out by yourself. I can't go further. My enemies might remember me." Demetre turned towards Tavin with a crooked smile. "It's been fun. Remember, don't trust anyone. There are no friends on the other side."

"Wait," Tavin reached towards Demetre remembering just in time not to touch him.

"Did you — did you really see my father cross over? Will I find him?"

Demetre's ghostly eyes were sad little holes of darkness. "He never came back, Tavin. It's not a good sign."

Tavin nodded, but couldn't quite squash the idea. At the very least, he decided, he could look around a little while he was there.

Demetre faded away into the gloom. A lump built in his throat but Tavin pushed it back.

With a destructive grin, Tavin dug into the wallpaper with his knife. He soon found the bumpy edges of a door hidden in the stairwell wall. Tavin tore a chunk of paper away. The aroma of mildew spread through the stairwell like heavy perfume. Tavin ripped more paper away from the wall, ignoring the fine rain of plaster and glue thickening the air. Finally, he'd pulled enough off to free edges of the door and tug it open.

The walls in the closet-sized room were black with grime and hung with dusty cobwebs. A narrow flight of stairs, with shallow handholds cut like nooks into each wooden step, crept up into total darkness. With a last glance over his shoulder, Tavin stepped into the tiny room and placed his hands on the lower handholds. The door closed behind him, shutting out the light.

Tavin felt his way slowly upward. Several times, he heard small things scurrying in the dark. When something ran lightly over his hand, he jerked his head in surprise and bit his tongue hard enough to taste blood.

The climb felt like it took hours. Tavin tried not to imagine what would happen if he fell. A few times, he forced himself to stop and take several deep calming breaths before going on. At last, he came to a place where there were no more handholds. Tavin groped blindly for a few panicky seconds until his fingers found the hard metal of a latch above him. He pushed upwards and pulled himself up into a wide empty room.

A skylight, jammed between leaning rafters, spilled fading light onto a wooden floor carpeted by fine dust. Thick curtains of cobwebs hung from the ceiling. The air was stale and heavy. At the far end of the room, a low green door seemed to wait expectantly for him.

Tavin walked warily forward, painfully aware of the footprints he tracked through the dust. A single line, printed carefully on dirty yellow paper and pinned up with a rusty tack, hung on the door.

Face your past, or turn on back

Tavin frowned, read the line once more and reached for the handle. As he touched the corroded metal, yellow sparks shot out from the door, knocking him backwards and onto the ground.

"Trust me, Tavin, this is for the best."

Clutching his chest and gasping, Tavin struggled to get up. He turned his head towards the speaker and his jaw dropped in shock.

His father stood square in the middle of the room, untouched by cobwebs or dust, his dark hair parted on the side and combed severely back: just the way Tavin remembered it.

"I'm not leaving" he continued, *"I'm exploring possibilities."*

Tavin shook himself. It wasn't real. It was a memory — the last time he'd seen his father.

His father bent down. His eyes looked right through Tavin.

"I need you to take care of Moreanna for me, Tavin," he said. *"She's a delicate flower; she won't survive without you to watch out for her."*

Tavin nodded unconsciously, just the way he had two years ago.

"When I get back I'll make it up to you. We'll be a family again. There's just something I need to do first." Tavin's father fixed him with a pointed gaze. *"Don't leave her, Tavin. She's special, you both are. She needs you."*

The memory blinked out, leaving Tavin unsteady on his feet. His breath slowed and his heart thudded heavily beneath his scar. Tavin stepped back from the door. It glowed blue around the edges. The paper on the door was gone, leaving behind a faint whiff of sulfur. Tavin swallowed.

"Nice try," he said, balling his hands into fists. "But it's not the same thing." Tavin felt the heat rise in his face. "I'm not my father. I'm not abandoning anyone, and I'm going to come back."

He grabbed the latch and pushed.

His body felt funny for a moment, his head buzzing like a TV channel without reception. His stomach slid sideways. Tavin walked forward — or thought he did — and stepped into someplace else.

The Shadowlands

Tavin stood upon a rooftop of a building that looked very much like the roof of his grandfather's farmhouse. The moon above him shone as bright as day; the shadow of the house in the courtyard below looked like a jagged hole, swallowing up anything that touched it.

Tavin dropped down on his hands and knees, inching away from the green door and towards the sharp peak of the roof, looking for a way down.

He frowned in doubt. He could see the crooked spire of the village church against the sky. He was supposed to be in another world but nothing had changed. For a brief second he wondered if it had all been some sort of joke.

Then he saw orange torchlights flickering in the street and a forbidding shiver crawled down his back. He looked again. All the buildings of the village were still in the places they should be, but everything else was wrong: crumbling, dark, and putrid.

Tavin reached the peak of the roof, crouching to avoid the wind.

"Stupid boy," said a voice. "This is no place for humans."

Tavin's foot slipped on a loose tile. He caught the top of the roof with his fingers and dug in for dear life. He looked up in disbelief.

The girl from the garden stood on the peak of the roof, balancing like an expert tightrope walker. Her eyes and mouth were two slashes of darkness.

Tavin could feel his temperature rise. He straddled the spine of the roof and dried his sweaty palms on his jeans. "Who are you?"

The girl ignored him, watching him with a hard glittering glare.

"I'm not going back," Tavin said. The wind picked up, forcing him to yell.

The girl's eyes seemed to glow. Her red hair whipped madly around her head. "Then you will die."

Tavin gritted his teeth and rose to a crouch. The wind buffeted him from both sides.

He locked his eyes upon the girl and, one foot at a time, edged towards her.

The girl backed away until her heels hung out over empty air. She never once took her eyes off him. Tavin heard a low thrumming sound and the air behind the girl began to shimmer. With a wicked smile, she stepped off the roof.

Tavin cried out in alarm, but instead of falling, the girl remained level with the roof, rocking with the wind. Tavin slipped left, banging his shin. Red shingles flew from beneath his feet and shattered in the courtyard below. Before he could recover, he was sliding down and gaining speed. He skidded over the red tile and slid over the edge of the roof with a yell of terror.

His heart roared in his ears; the shadows of the courtyard filled his vision. Then something yanked him from above, jerking his shirt tight across his chest and against his throat. The bottom of his jacket swept the cobblestone and he careened towards the corner of the farmyard in a crazy pendulum swing.

Tavin caught a glance of the girl above him. She gripped him with both hands by his collar, her expression strained.

"The wall!" Tavin yelled. "You're going to hit the wall!"

She said something nasty. They pulled up, barely clearing the tall wall surrounding the courtyard.

The wind picked them up, sweeping them beyond the village. Darkness howled with rage and bent the barley nearly flat. The girl cried out and Tavin heard something tear. They dropped towards the ground, flying sideways like a jet coming to land. Tavin's shoulder hit first. He skidded along his side and rolled head over heels through the grain. When he finally stopped, Tavin had to squeeze his eyes shut against the view of the sky spinning above him, fighting to keep from being sick.

Tavin took several slow breaths and waited for the dizziness to abate before opening his eyes again. The pressure on his chest turned out to be the girl. Tavin wrapped his arm carefully over her shoulders, his nostrils filling with the scent of warm blackberries.

Two shimmering blue wings lay flat upon her back. At Tavin's touch, they fluttered weakly and the wind tugged spitefully at the large tears. Tavin felt a stab of guilt. The girl's beautiful wings hung in tatters, all because he'd been too stupid to take his time on the slippery roof.

"Hey, are you okay?"

The girl jerked awake. A dagger appeared in her hand as she scrambled off him.

"Wait! Stop!" Tavin thrust his palm forward. "I don't want to fight!"

The girl narrowed her eyes. She pulled her lips back from her teeth and flashed a pair of pointy fangs at him.

"I — uh," Tavin fumbled for his words as he stared at the fangs.

The girl's grimace turned to a wide disconcerting smile. "I am Aria," she said.

"Good ... I'm, uh ... my name's Tavin." Tavin climbed to his feet. His palms were beginning to sweat again. "I'm not going to hurt you, okay? You can put the knife away."

She wrinkled her nose, but slid the knife into a sheath strapped to her wrist. "You're a human," she said.

"Call me Tavin. And you are … um, what are you exactly?" Now that the knife was out of sight, Tavin felt free to study the rest of her. She wore dark leggings and a black shirt that fit snuggly across her round chest and hips. He noticed with relief that a pale gray harness strapped around her shoulders, waist and legs held her wings on. At least the ruined wings didn't hurt her.

Tavin, his cheeks burning in the dark, looked again. There wasn't a loose inch of cloth anywhere on her. Leather straps tied down the tall moccasins she wore to make her boots as close fitting as the rest of her. He supposed the tight suit was practical for flying, but all he could think about was the leather outfit Catwoman liked to wear as she chased after Batman.

Aria flashed her teeth again. She began to pace. "I'm a fairy," she said. "We're much more powerful than humans."

Tavin swallowed. "I need your help."

Aria cocked her head. "You're not as ugly as everyone says. Is it true that humans grow hair on their faces?"

"Only grown men."

Aria made a face. "That's disgusting."

Tavin wiped his hands on his jeans. "Please," he said. "My sister might be dying; I came here to find a cure."

She walked in a slow circle, her movements dangerous, her scent intoxicating. She stopped inches from his face and ran a cool finger down the side of his chin. "No one crosses over," she said. "There is a treaty. You stay on your side, we stay on ours."

Tavin shook off her hand, refusing to be distracted. No matter how pretty she was, he wouldn't let her get in the way of helping Moreanna. "That's not good enough," he said. "You crossed over, I saw you."

Aria's expression turned sour. "I don't have to explain myself to a human."

Now it was Tavin's turn to smile. "You're curious about me, aren't you?"

Aria crossed her arms. "Who would be curious about a stinky human?"

Tavin's grin grew bolder. "I think you are. That's why you saved me from falling."

Aria narrowed her eyes. "You know nothing. I told you, there is a treaty. Maybe I stopped a war by saving you."

"It's more than that," Tavin replied, enjoying himself. "I can sense things and you're going to help me. I can already tell."

"I have magic," Aria snapped her teeth. "I am strong and you are weak. Why should I help you?"

Tavin shrugged. "Have it your way." He picked a direction at random and began to push through the barley. A line of dark trees edged the star-studded horizon. He figured they would be as good a place to start as any.

At his back Tavin heard Aria release a sting of rough-sounding words in a long fluid hiss.

Her cool fingers closed around his arm and pulled him to a stop. "I want a new knife," she said. "I want a sharp one that will not rust. You humans have such things."

Tavin shrugged again. "No problem — if you help me find a cure."

"I want something else." She moved in close; so close, her nose almost bumped his chin.

Tavin sucked in a breath. "What?"

Aria's green eyes bored into his. "Sanctuary," she said.

"You want to leave the Shadowlands?"

"Etheria," she said. "Shadowlands is a human word. Etheria means jewel."

"Why do you want to leave?"

Her face was stony. "It's too much to explain to a human. Give me your oath or I leave you now."

She was definitely bigger than a kitten. He could already see the look on his sister's face when he brought a strange girl with fangs into their little apartment. On the other hand, maybe she could stay with his grandparents. He almost laughed aloud at the thought.

Tavin shook his head. What choice did he really have? He'd just have to work out the details later. Tavin slid a sidelong glance at Aria, once again soaking in the effect of her harnessed uniform. He supposed it could be worse.

"I promise," he said. He held out a hand. Aria, after staring at his hand for a puzzled moment, reached out and gave his fingers a tight squeeze. She smiled.

"I do not know how to cure your sister, but I can bring you to someone who does." Aria flashed her teeth again. "We must go back to the village," she said. "Into the heart of Goblintown."

The village reared towards the sky, crumbling and ancient. Doors and windows hung askew. Dead vines clung to the sides of houses like an epitaph on a gravestone. The entire village smelled of rotten meat. The streets leaked puddles of something dark and sticky.

Aria's grin was pointy. "You're not afraid?"

"No." Tavin's face reddened and he wondered if fairies could hear heartbeats. "What is this place?"

"Do you not know it?"

"It's like the village my grandparents live in, but — " The smell of something putrid hit him in the face and Tavin doubled over, covering his nose as he dry heaved.

"Humans call our world the Shadowlands because our worlds are so similar. Our worlds are like mirrors, but here ..." Aria smirked but

Tavin thought he saw something sad move behind her eyes. "… Here the sun doesn't shine so bright."

She turned her head, her nostrils flaring wide. "Quiet! Against the wall!"

They darted into the gloom of a leaning building, pressing their backs tight against the slimy wall. A large, round-shouldered creature, with footsteps like raw meat slapping against stone, lumbered around the corner of a house. It dragged something heavy and metallic. Aria hissed softly and dumped a handful of slime onto Tavin's head.

"Wha — "

She leaned an elbow against his throat and pressed her small hand over his mouth. "Rub it into your hair, human, or I leave you to die."

Tavin, biting his tongue to stop himself from gagging, did as she asked. Aria scooped more slime from the walls and smeared it on his face and across the front of his jacket for good measure. The creature came closer. Tavin could hear it drooling. The metal thing it dragged glinted cold blue in the moonlight. It was an axe, as long as a reaper's scythe, stained black along its edge.

There were no windows or doors to dash through. The wall was too slippery to climb. Tavin's breath caught in his throat. He clenched his teeth so hard he was sure he cracked a filling.

The thing, as if lead by some supernatural hand, seemed to know exactly where they were. It clumped to the middle of the street and stopped directly across from them, squinting with its beady yellow eyes into the shadows. For the first time, Tavin was able to get a clear view of the creature, and the truth of what he saw drove his mind to a place of horror he had never known existed.

It wore a dress: a paisley print, stained and torn, with stockings and a yellow wig.

The creature's reptilian flesh erupted from the bottom of the stockings like toxic waste from a sewer pipe. The wig rolled down over the creature's fat head like hot custard. Its jowls moved with soundless stupidity and glinted with a smear of red lipstick.

Tavin shuddered, unsure if he should throw up or faint. Aria's blade whispered against cloth as she slid it from her belt and widened her stance.

Just when Tavin thought the suspense would drive him mad, and he was considering jumping out of the shadows and screaming 'nice sweet meat,' a sharp clang further on down the street caused the creature to turn its head with a happy grunt. It sniffed once more at the shadowy wall, turned and lumbered eagerly away.

Aria waited a full minute before easing away from the house. Tavin followed her, his legs unsteady. He gagged again as he scraped at his hair with his fingernails. The slime had already begun to go crusty. "Okay, there's something I need to know."

Aria slid her dagger away with a snap of her wrist and set her hands upon her hips. "What?"

Tavin shuddered. "What was with the dress?"

"All goblins dress up. They believe they're a human tribe under a curse. Any more questions?"

"Humans? Really?"

"They say that they were once the strongest and most beautiful of all the humans, until a human mage put a curse on them to stop them from ruling your world. They dress in human clothes and try to mimic human life but they are just monsters. No one really believes the curse story." Aria shrugged. "Throw them rotting meat and they're nothing but teeth. Now stay quiet — and try not to smell so human."

Aria tossed her head with a smirk and stepped out into the flickering shadows of the street. Tavin followed as quietly as he could, trying to guess what humans smelt like.

Aria lead them down narrow alleyways and hidden paths over rubble. Despite the orange lights that flickered ominously behind closed shutters and the lumbering scuffling noises that chased them around every corner, they made it across town without seeing any more goblins. They stopped on the edge of a cemetery bordered by a high wall and tucked against an old church. A heavy iron gate, oozing mist, hung crookedly across the entrance.

Cold wind crawled its way down Tavin's neck. When he was younger, he'd always liked cemeteries: a graveyard had been a safe quiet place that he could go and not be bothered. Ever since the death of his mother, though, he'd stayed away. The thought of his beautiful mother rotting away in the earth — just another buried corpse among hundreds — was one he couldn't bear. His eyes burned suspiciously into Aria's back.

"Why a graveyard?" he asked. "There's only dead people in there."

The gate screeched loudly as Aria shouldered it open, causing them both to wince. "Who said we're looking for someone who's alive?" she whispered harshly. "Now are you coming or not?"

The graveyard rose before them in lumpy hills like cold porridge. Gravestones — gray smears in the dark — crested the hills in crooked rows. Tavin ground his teeth and stepped through the gate.

If he looked too long at one spot, Tavin thought he could see shadows flittering between the stones. He heard soft rustling sounds coming from all directions and hoped it was nothing more than falling leaves.

They wound their way through the maze of tombstones, crumbling monuments and cavernous mausoleums. Angels carved in weathered stone watched them with shadowed eyes and broken wings. Weeping willows bent low over the path and ivy snaked up and over everything. Rotting black elm and chestnut trees leaned low over their heads, crowding each other as if trying to get a better look at the two intruders.

Aria halted in front of a round clearing hemmed in closely by tall bushes and draped in thick cobwebs. She reached out a hand and pointed, her voice nearly lost in the rustle of holly leaves.

"There."

Tavin looked.

A worn, life-sized statue of a young girl stood in the middle of the clearing. Dressed in a veil of glittering moonlit cobwebs, she watched them; her palms turned upwards in entreaty.

Tavin whistled softly. "That looks old."

"She is." Aria cleared her throat. "Lucy's older than this graveyard, older than the great war. She was here before my family came to stay in this area."

Aria hesitated. "She's not what you think she is."

A shiver ran down Tavin's back.

"She used to be human," continued Aria. "She had a special gift — sometimes humans do." Aria looked sidelong at Tavin. "Lucy could see the future. She saw things centuries before they happened; and she saw something that scared her. No one knows what it was, but it was bad enough that Lucy worked a spell to turn herself into a statue. Some people think she will wake again to help us fight the very last war."

Tavin let out a shaky breath of relief. "So she's not dead."

Aria shook her head. "I think she's somewhere in-between. She sees the dead, but she's here at the same time, watching us."

"What do I do?" he asked.

Aria took a step back. "Ask her," she said. "She already knows you're here."

Tavin stared at the statue. The movement of the bushes behind her played tricks with his eyes. Had she shifted slightly? Did her head just move or was that another trick of the light?

Cold mist wrapped his ankles in shackles. A sweet, sickly scent, like rotten roses, tickled his nose. Tavin knew he should turn back, but found himself unable to. He took another step forward. A shaft of clean moonlight fell upon the statue's stone face, revealing the faint shape of a star etched on the girl's forehead. Then her head really did move, and Tavin noticed her eyes had no pupils.

"Tavin."

He yelled with fright and jumped back. He landed awkwardly and turned his ankle upon a rock. Tentacles of darkness flowed swiftly down and out from the statue's open arms. They wrapped about his chest, his wrists, his ankles and even his head. The darkness lifted him into the air.

"Tavin," said the voice. "Don't be afraid."

Tavin thrashed in terror as shadow tentacles reached inside and touched his soul. He screamed, feeling his chest burst open.

"Tavin."

The pain stopped. Tavin opened his eyes.

"Where am I?" he asked. Soft red light pulsed from every direction. He stood in a small room. The walls heaved as if they were breathing.

Lucy stood before him: a girl with blond hair and wide blank eyes. She raised a hand, brushing her fingertips across his face. Her touch brought with it the feeling of deep biting cold.

"What do you seek?" she asked.

Tavin took a slow breath, tightening his hands into fists to stop them from shaking. "I need to know about my sister. Tell me how I can save her."

Lucy cocked her head. "Your sister's restoration is close. The answer is within."

Tavin frowned. "What do I have to do?"

She pressed a white finger to his chest. "You bear the mark, you must use it."

Tavin pulled away from her cold touch. "That's an old burn."

"Tavin, look at me," Lucy said. She pressed forward, running her cold fingers across his face, around his eyes and down his throat. "You are not your father," she said. "You are more. Where he failed, you will succeed. Have faith. There is darkness in you, but it has not overcome."

"My father — ," Tavin's voice scraped roughly past his throat. "Tell me what happened to him."

She closed her eyes for a moment. "He is alive. He has travelled far to the east. He searches for something; his quest consumes him." Lucy opened her eyes. "He draws close to what he seeks, but he has already forgotten why."

"Will he come home?"

Lucy's sightless eyes gazed into his soul. "No."

Tavin gritted his teeth. "I don't know what to do with what you're telling me. I don't understand."

Lucy reached up and cupped Tavin's face in her hands. This time, desperate for an answer he could use, Tavin didn't pull back. Her cold touch leached warmth from him as if taking life.

"Listen closely to my words. Your sister's life depends on it." Lucy smiled with frostbitten lips. Her pale hair began to move around her face as if caught by wind. "Evil draws near. Two universes: two sides of the same coin. What happens in one is echoed in another. A world of magic and a world of creation." Lucy's voice moved like dried leaves on dead branches. "The black sword awakes; its foe draws near. The Elements awake, breaking to his will. Through chaos, by fire, he returns." Lucy turned her head, her blank eyes cutting into him like laser beams. "The Unmaker is coming!"

Tavin awoke with a gasp, falling hard to the ground and tumbling through the mist.

A hand, burning like fire, touched his face.

"You're cold," Aria said. She sounded upset. "You shouldn't be cold like that."

Tavin curled into a ball. Lucy's words screeched across his brain like fingers on a chalkboard. "He's coming back."

"Who?"

"The Unmaker." Tavin's tongue felt like a stone.

An odd look crossed Aria's face. Her eyes widened in alarm.

Tavin climbed unsteadily to his feet. "I think — I think I have to find him," he said.

"You're not well," Aria replied. "You're speaking nonsense. Hang on to me. I'll bring you home."

Madame Caveat

He hated life itself. He destroyed with a touch and absorbed any magic thrown at him. He'd murdered thousands.

He was dead.

Or at least, she thought he was.

Aria wrapped her arms tightly around Tavin's waist, half carrying him as they hobbled towards the cemetery gate. She felt a sharp pang of regret. Humans were more fragile than she realized. She shouldn't have brought him.

Whatever was wrong, Aria would bet her wings there wasn't a human hospital on earth to help him.

The Unmaker. Again, his name invaded her thoughts.

Aria shivered. Only a handful of creatures remained alive who had walked the world during the time of terror. Their stories were fantastic. They talked of a being, cloaked in darkness, with red eyes and diseased skin. They could not bribe him with power or buy him with gold. He wanted nothing but the destruction of the world. He had been nearly unstoppable.

Tavin stumbled on a stone, throwing them both down onto the gravel path. Aria pulled him back up. She growled.

The human needed magical healing, but if her father ever found out she'd been helping a human, she'd be grounded — literally — for the rest of her life. She hissed. With her out of the way, there'd be nobody left to stand up to her brother, and that was a possibility she'd rather die than face.

She hesitated, unsure what to do. The crooked tombstones and rattling willow branches almost seemed friendly.

They rounded a bend in the path and the light changed, flickering across the ground in red and orange hues. Silhouetted black against the red light, Aria recognized the lumpy shapes jostling each other near the cemetery walls.

She said something ugly. The good thing about being descended from an ancient fairy race was that you knew all the best swear words. Being grounded was no longer the problem; it was the rest of her life she was worried about now.

"What is it?" Tavin asked.

Aria growled, exposing her fangs. She scanned for another exit but the dark masses crowded against every inch of the wall. "Goblins," she said. "They've woken up."

Their eyes were bulged and bloodshot, their skin sagging and warty. Long strings of drool hung in gooey strands from their jaws and mucus leaked from their noses. Most of them wore tatters of human clothing, torn and ill fitting. In their knobby hands they clutched clubs, pitchforks, and knives. Tall, fat, short, and skinny, goblins came in all shapes and sizes. What they shared in common was razor sharp teeth and a taste for live screaming flesh.

Tavin fell to his knees. Aria knelt, supporting him against her as she slid out of her harness and began calling magic from the air to mend the holes in her wings. Tendrils of soft blue magic streamed from her fingers and began to knit together the worst of the tears. Aria wiped her forehead nervously with her shirtsleeve. It was taking too long.

The goblins had seen the glimmer of magic. A loud howl of anger rose. Some of the bigger ones gathered the courage to climb over the cemetery wall, where they stood drooling and blinking nervously. Goblins rarely dared to disturb the dead, but they hated intruders on their territory even more than they hated bad luck. More goblins began climbing the wall.

The wings glittered with life. With an exclamation of triumph, Aria struggled back into the straps. The airflow felt funny, but they worked. Aria wrapped her arms around Tavin and pulled him onto his feet. The closest goblins began scooping up and eating handfuls of dirt, their shirtsleeves dragging through the mud. They would come just as soon as they believed the graveyard spirits were appeased. Unfortunately, ritual dirt scarfing never took long.

Aria's wings began to hum.

Tavin's eyes focused for a moment. They'd faded from dark brown to a sickly gray color.

"What are you doing?" he asked.

"Don't worry, this'll work," she said, her voice straining. "Don't let go."

Fairies never sweat, but they do glow on occasion. Aria began beaming like a headlight. The burly dirt-eaters, now finished their grimy meal, spat chunks of mud. With busting seams and popping buttons, they roared and lumbered towards them.

Inch by inch Aria began to lift. Air whistled through the repaired tears but the magical stitching held. They climbed a foot, then three, then seven. Her wings hummed like a small hurricane, glistening fairy glow beaded down her face. Grubby goblin hands clawed upwards, only inches beneath their dangling feet.

Aria felt a slipstream coming. "Hang on!" she yelled. "This is going to be rough!"

They lurched down and to the right, kicking as many goblin heads as they could manage. The slipstream yanked them upwards and Aria launched them off the edge of an angel's wing.

They shot up, crossing over the wall of the cemetery. The entire goblin horde turned and ran after them.

"Look at all the pretty lights!" Tavin murmured.

Aria almost dropped him on a matter of principle.

With sharp popping sounds, the wings began to tear under the strain. Aria and Tavin fell into a spinning corkscrew towards the edge of Goblintown. Sloping houses shot past in a dizzy red-roofed blur. Aria threw her weight towards the tall church spire. She caught a hold of the steeple, sending them like a stone from a slingshot hurtling up towards the moon. They spun in fast circles over the grassy fields, rapidly leaving Goblintown and its inhabitants behind. The real danger now came from the cold storm winds beyond the village.

The storm buffeted them from all sides, throwing them back and forth like a soccer ball at a little-league game. Howling air currents picked them up and threw them violently into a dark grove of pines on the edge of the forest.

Aria and Tavin crashed though the thorny branches. Gasping for breath, Aria opened her wings wide, kicking off the trees and fighting for altitude.

Tavin lost his grip.

Aria dove and tried to catch him but she missed. Tavin crashed through the trees. His limp body bent a branch and it sprung back towards Aria, striking her across the face. White light exploded before her eyes, turning the world into a confusing jumble of black and gray shapes.

Tavin, where are you? I can't feel you! You're so far away!

Tavin opened his eyes. Jagged black treetops sliced into the moonlit sky like broken knives. He breathed.

I'm here. His breath crystallized into a cloud before his face. He pushed himself upright. His heart labored inside his chest, struggling to feed life to the rest of him. His hands were white, his nails a dark purple color. Deep cold gnawed into his bones and slowed his blood as it labored through his veins.

For a moment — I thought — , Moreanna's tone sounded panicked. *Something's wrong with you Tavin, I can feel it. Who's the Unmaker? Tavin, you need to stop what you're doing, you need to come home.*

Not yet. Tavin stood, scanning the bushes he'd fallen upon and the trees beyond with careful deliberation. The moonlight that seeped through the branches was misty and dim. His uncertain footsteps made no noise on the needled ground.

"Aria! Can you hear me?" The trees absorbed Tavin's calls and returned them with stifling silence.

He passed a small pool of water and knelt for a drink. As soon as he touched its surface, the water froze. The speed of the transformation caused the ice to crack, splitting the pool right down the center.

Tavin looked at the ice with an odd feeling of removal. It was like the time Demetre had frozen his voice so he couldn't cry out — only much worse. Lucy's touch had drawn away nearly all of his living warmth. Each beat of his heart felt slower than the last. He didn't have much time. He knew it with every breath he drew.

Everything's going to be okay, he told his sister. *Get some rest and stop bugging me.*

Please come back home, she said. Her voice faded away.

Tavin stood. He needed a plan. He'd lost his only friend in this world; if he was going to do anything for Moreanna before he died, he needed to find Aria. Strangely, his emotions felt as numb as his heart. Even the thought of death didn't frighten him. Instead, a part of him longed for the peaceful darkness that waited for him.

Tavin walked away from the frozen pool and towards a grove of close fir trees. As he reached out to push aside a branch, something sticky entangled his fingers. It was a thin gray rope, as thick around as his thumb. It froze beneath his touch and he snapped the thread, easily pulling his hand free.

Tavin frowned in puzzlement. Something about the rope stirred a memory, but he couldn't quite place it. He looked up and spotted several more strands weaving their way through the trees. He was just about to turn around and head in the opposite direction when something sharp pricked him in the back of his neck.

Tavin's stomach rolled with nausea and he fell forward onto his face.

He had to save Moreanna. He needed to find Aria.

But he couldn't feel his arms or legs.

Morry, he thought.

"Oh dear! Oh dear!" exclaimed a squeaky voice. "A human child! A sick human child!"

Tavin's eyes wouldn't focus. A blurry blob leaned over him and fussed.

"Don't worry my dear," said the blob. "I have you now. I'm going to take very good care of you!"

Tavin awoke beneath a mountain of quilts in a small round cottage. A small furry creature with a green collar — something like a mouse but with bigger ears — perched on his stomach and studied him with bright curious eyes.

A clay fireplace squatted in the middle of the hut, a pot bubbling merrily over the fire. Balls of yarn spilled across the floor, their bright strings hanging from the rafters in a dizzying tangle. Not far from his bed, an old woman sat in a battered rocking chair, knitting from the gigantic ball at her feet.

Tavin reached towards the creature on his belly. It scolded him with a sharp squeal and darted off the bed.

The old woman looked up. "Oh, you must not be so hasty to rise my dear," her voice was small and squeaky. "You are very sick."

She was right. As soon as the covers fell off, the chill hit. Tavin shivered and pulled the blankets tightly around his shoulders. "My — my friend," he said. "I think she's hurt."

The old woman put her knitting aside and stood. A large lump upon her back stooped her so low that her wrinkled, swollen hands hung below her knees. She wore layers of patterned shawls, some tied about her face and piled on top of her head. Her nose was large and crooked, her eyes small and bright. Every part of skin not covered was brown and creased with hundreds of fine wrinkles.

She smiled, revealing a black rotten grin. "You may call me Madame Caveat, my dear boy," she said. "I will look for your friend just as soon as you have some stew. You, my dear, must not go out. You are sick and it's dangerous in the dark woods."

Her wobbly old-lady voice was calming. She patted Tavin on the head and spooned stew for him into a rough wooden bowl. It was lumpy and gray but the smell made Tavin's mouth water. He remembered that he hadn't eaten anything since yesterday, and began spooning the stew ravenously into his mouth.

Madame Caveat watched him approvingly.

"I do so like to watch you young ones eat!" she chirped. "It does an old body good to see you well fed and happy. You'll be well enough soon, I don't doubt."

Tavin's head felt as heavy and thick as the stew he'd just eaten. It was too much work to talk anymore. He smiled sleepily before falling into a deep dream.

He awoke some hours later. The many blankets no longer warmed him, but at least his head felt clear.

Nothing remained of the fire but a few dimly glowing coals. The gloom did strange things to the cottage. It looked sinister and twisted. The strings of yarn hung like the tattered threads of a spider web.

Tavin let out a breath and watched it fog the air. His body felt numb, but he hardly minded. He climbed out of bed, and tugged on his jacket.

A flurry of movement rushed past him and stopped before the door. The small mouse creature reared onto its hind legs and began to chatter urgently.

Thinking of Pip, Tavin dug into his pockets. He found a few crumbled cookie crumbs and knelt to the ground.

"Here you go little guy, I'll bet you've never tried chocolate before!"

He held out his hand. The small creature cocked its head and jumped forward onto Tavin's foot. Tavin fell back in surprise and the creature bit down, its sharp front teeth slicing clean through his sneaker. Tavin yelped in surprise and kicked his foot out, sending the creature flying across the room. With an angry screech the creature landed on the far wall, held there with tiny talons on its hands and feet. It glared at Tavin and hissed before scurrying down the wall into the shadows.

"What a nasty little thing you are!" Tavin said. "I don't even want to know what she feeds you." Tavin looked down at his foot. Dark blood oozed slowly through the canvas of his shoe, but he felt no pain. He chewed his lip and decided it didn't matter.

Find Aria. Tavin left the hut with those words beating a tattoo through his brain. He found it hard to think about anything else. As he walked, he left frosty footsteps upon the grass. He hadn't wandered far when he spotted a hunched figure moving among the trees.

Madame Caveat sang quietly to herself. Curious, Tavin leaned against a tree, watching her cluck and chatter, fussing over something she'd found. She bent down in a pool of starlight and Tavin glimpsed a gray rabbit quivering in the bushes at her feet.

Madame Caveat made a queer little chuckle and Tavin pressed his hand against his mouth to stifle a gasp of horror. From under the pile of shawls upon her back, four long black spider legs unfolded and extended. On the end of each leg was a single talon. Faster than the strike of a scorpion, two of the four legs shot forward and pinned the rabbit to the ground.

Tavin had never heard a rabbit make noise. Its screams brought his heart up into his throat. He trembled, aching in horror, unable to look away.

Madame Caveat's black eyes glittered wickedly as she watched her helpless prey thrash. The rabbit's body swelled grotesquely. Madame Caveat shifted, blocking Tavin's view of what happened next.

He leaned shakily back against the tree. Madame Caveat folded her spider legs back beneath her pile of shawls. Crooning happily to herself, she continued on her way.

With halting steps, Tavin made his way to the place the rabbit lay. The truth was worse than he imagined.

The small corpse lay in a pool of pulpy gore, an empty sack of skin and fur. Everything: its bones, all of its internal organs, even its eyes were gone. He saw an ugly red puncture wound, like an open sore, on the rabbit's neck. Then the smell hit his nostrils, and Tavin began dry heaving. Despite his condition, a clammy sweat broke out on Tavin's forehead, freezing into small crystal drops.

The rabbit had been sucked dry.

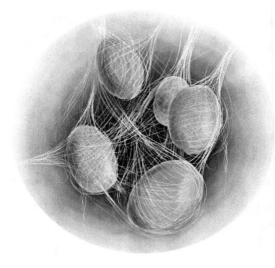

Spiderweave

*C*avin hurried away from the corpse as quickly as his cold limbs and struggling lungs allowed. He hugged his stomach and wiped his mouth, trying to forget the sweet dead smell of Madame Caveat's liquefied kill.

Sticky cords wove themselves densely between the tree trunks. Some strands were as fine as silk thread, others thicker than his bicep. They froze and shattered at his touch, making sharp cracking noises.

Tavin ran deeper into the forest. Find Aria, find Aria, find Aria, screamed his brain. Grey cobweb veils ensnared the tops of the trees, falling to drape the ground in sticky residue. He began to see cocoons suspended off the ground like meat in a butcher's shop.

And then he spotted her.

She hung thirty feet up in the heart of a gigantic spider web. Her dark red hair fell in tragic strands around her pale face. Her wings hung in pieces above her.

Fear coursed through him. "Aria!"

She stirred. Her eyes opened and flashed like emeralds. She struggled against the web that held her bound with a curse.

"Aria!" Tavin repeated. "I'm here!"

"Tavin?" Her voice scraped roughly from her throat. "Tavin!" Her eyes widened. "Get me down!"

Tavin grabbed a strand of webbing, causing it to shiver and stiffen as it froze. He gave it a kick and the strand shattered. Tavin grabbed a second strand, snapping it with his hands. Aria clutched at the web as she fell, slowing her tumble to the ground.

She struggled uncertainly to her feet, eyeing Tavin warily. "Thank you," she said hoarsely.

Aria slapped her arms and legs, grinding her teeth as the blood began to flow. She studied him from the corner of her vision. "You don't look so good."

Tavin looked down. A dusting of ice covered his clothing. The icy grass crunched beneath his feet like granola. Tavin smiled weakly, his wan expression freezing into place.

"I'm glad I found you."

He suddenly felt tired; his arms seemed impossibly heavy. He'd done it. He'd saved her, and now he could rest.

Aria slapped him. "Wake up!" Tavin frowned and opened his eyes. He'd almost fallen asleep.

Aria slapped him again. "Do something, get angry! Tavin," Aria said, "listen to me. The sickness makes you not care about anything. You have to fight it."

Tavin backed away a couple steps. He shook his head as if having trouble focusing his eyes. "I like it when you use my name," he said. He'd forgotten about something, something important. He sat down on a log, trying to remember.

Aria looked scared. He'd seen her face goblins without flinching, but whatever she saw when she looked at him shook her to the core.

"I didn't mean it," she said. "I didn't know Lucy would do this. I just thought she could tell you how to cure your sister."

Moreanna. Tavin looked up. "I have to save her." Deep in his stomach, he felt a flicker of warmth.

"Yes," Aria gripped his arm. "You have to save her, Tavin. No one else can."

Tavin clenched his teeth and rose slowly to his feet. He noticed two spots of color high upon Aria's cheeks. He did his best to grin. "Don't worry, it'll work out."

A loud shriek ripped through the night. Aria cringed and covered her ears.

"Who dares? Who dares break my web?"

Tavin twisted around, placing himself between Aria and the voice.

Madame Caveat hung high in a tree. All four of her spider legs secured her to the trunk while her fat bloated body swung freely in space. She hissed and cursed, gnashing her black teeth, her many shawls fluttering behind her.

Aria snarled. "You!"

Madame Caveat shrieked. It was hard to tell if it was fear or laughter. "Little fairy," she hissed, "a sweet little female."

Aria's eyes narrowed. She crouched slightly and tightened her fists. "Monster!"

Tavin looked from Madame Caveat to Aria, the image of the liquefied rabbit still fresh in his mind. "Aria, forget it. Let's get out of here."

Aria growled, shaking her head. "Never," she said, her eyes fixed on Madame Caveat. "I know this creature. She's one of the Chill clan: a murderer."

Madame Caveat leaped from one tree to another amidst a whirl of tattered cloth, her black eyes glittering. "Mine, mine, mine!" she screeched. "Those caught in the web are mine, their blood is mine!"

"Aria!" The warmth in Tavin's belly spread upward into his chest. His heartbeat spiked and he felt strength flow into his arms.

Aria's fingertips began to glow with blue light.

With a shriek of triumph, Madame Caveat leapt through the air towards them. Her mouth opened and thick strands of webbing shot out of her throat, striking the ground and solidifying as Aria and Tavin scrambled out of the way.

Madame Caveat swung around in a wide circle, spewing webbing from several directions. Aria traced a symbol in the air and pulled two glowing swords from the centre. She spun, deflecting the webbing and charring it to fine ash.

Tavin froze in surprise and nearly fell over. He stared at Aria in open-mouthed awe.

Caveat hissed and dropped lower. Aria, seeing her chance, lunged forward to intercept her. She dodged the sticky fluid and slashed Madame Caveat's side with a sword. Madame Caveat fell heavily to the ground, yellow mucus seeping from her wound.

As Aria closed in for the kill, Madame Caveat reared up, her eyes red with rage. She charged, using her long legs to get past the reach of Aria's swords.

A claw, dripping with venom, sliced downwards. Aria dove to the side, rolling desperately to avoid the poisoned strike.

Fire ripped through Tavin's veins, his mind filled with wrath. He leapt forward between Aria and Madame Caveat. Madame Caveat's claw slashed through his jacket sleeve, narrowly missing the flesh of his arm. Tavin didn't even notice.

"Don't you dare touch her!" he screamed. His hand shot out and he caught a hold of Caveat's spider leg.

Madame Caveat shrieked in pain, her leg freezing at Tavin's touch. Aria, back on her feet, darted in with her swords, slicing deeply across Madame Caveat's thigh. Tavin twisted his wrist with a jerk. Madame Caveat shrieked again, her frozen leg snapped off at its lower joint.

Cursing and weeping, Madame Caveat leapt free and scrambled up into the trees.

Aria dropped her blades, short of breath and grinning. "I knew you could do it, Tavin! Welcome back."

Tavin didn't feel quite so ready to celebrate. Icy cold crept into his limbs like a bad omen.

He thrashed his arms about, trying to get some feeling back.

"Where'd she go?" he asked. His gaze darted uneasily from one tree to the next. "That can't be it."

A rustle in the trees warned them. Tavin's head shot up; Aria yelled and jumped aside. Before Tavin could react, Madame Caveat dropped from above, pinning him beneath her bloated weight.

"Tavin!" Aria ran forward, slashing with her swords. Yellow mucus burst out from Caveat's wounds, burning Aria's hands like acid. The swords vanished and Caveat spun, knocking Aria back with a powerful blow from one of her spider legs.

Tavin ground his teeth and tried to rise. Tight strands of webbing hardened across his arms and chest. They froze as they touched Tavin's hands but he couldn't move to break the cocoon in time. Madame Caveat spewed more webbing, layering it until Tavin's chest labored beneath the weight.

At that moment, a small earthquake rumbled across the forest floor. The icy cocoon cracked, but didn't break.

Madame Caveat backed up nervously, her old lady head spinning around on her shoulders as she tried to find the source of the tremor.

Another rumble passed through the earth.

With a shriek, Madame Caveat leapt straight up, scrambling into the sanctuary of the trees.

Aria ran towards Tavin. He coughed, struggling to draw shallow breaths.

"What was that?" he asked.

"I don't know," Aria replied.

She dropped to her knees and ran her hands anxiously across Tavin's icy prison. "Watch the trees in case she comes back."

Tavin nodded, scanning the dark world above them. Aria traced a symbol through the air and a glowing sword formed in her hands. She pressed the blade forward, the cocoon beginning to melt beneath its blue glow.

Tavin managed a weak grin. "Why in the world do you want a knife if you can pull glowing swords out of thin air?"

A small smile crept up the corner of Aria's mouth. "A knife is sneakier in the dark," she said. "No one sees it coming."

Tavin's shiver had nothing to do with the cold. Somehow, he didn't think she was joking. "You went a little bit crazy back there," he said. "You know that, don't you?"

Aria shrugged. "You were the one who jumped in front of her."

"To protect you."

"Who says I need — ow!" Aria yelped. She raised her free hand to her face. A drop of purple blood welled up on the tip of one of her fingers.

Tavin's muscles tensed. "What happened?"

Aria looked uncertain.

"A spider bite," her voice grew faint. "A little spider bit me." Aria's skin took on a pale greenish color.

Her sword vanished and her eyes filmed over.

She slumped to the ground.

A thin laugh echoed through the trees. Madame Caveat began to sing in a wheedling voice.

Little fly, in my web
Now you're mine,
Soon you're dead!

Tavin fought against his bonds with renewed strength. "Caveat!" he yelled, "don't you dare come closer!"

The singing drew near.

Madame Caveat appeared merrily among the trees, rocking on a thread. Her mouth dripped with black poison.

"I'm warning you," Tavin ground his teeth and strained against his bonds. The ice weakened and cracked further. He pulled his legs beneath him and pushed.

"Settle down, precious," Madame Caveat said. "You've been very sick today." She leapt from the tree. Webbing shot from her mouth and encased Tavin's legs. She dropped more fluid across his chest.

Tavin gasped as his ribs cracked and his lungs compressed. A ball of webbing hardened in his mouth.

Madame Caveat gathered Aria close, wrapping her in a flexible cocoon. Tavin growled in fury, his cry muffled by the webbing.

The earth shook again, followed closely by the rumbling sound of hoof beats.

Madame Caveat hissed and dropped her prey. Her poisoned talons waved in defiance as she squinted into the shadows of the trees. The ground beneath them began to roll like a boiling pot. The grassy bubbles erupted, rocks tearing free to hang suspended in the air.

"Who dares?" Madame Caveat said. "She is my right! Mine!"

A magnificent white stag burst from the trees like a shaft of pure moonlight. On his back rode a man with a long dark jacket and a tall staff. Both the staff and the rider's hands crackled with green fire.

The man jumped from the back of the stag and slammed his staff to the ground. The floating rocks hurtled inward towards Madame Caveat. The earth shook more violently than ever and the webbing that bound Tavin fractured and crumbled to dust.

Madame Caveat shrieked, cowering beneath the barrage of stones. The white stag leapt forward in a streak of silver. Madame Caveat backed against a tree, her talons menacing. She spat black slime.

Light enveloped the stag. His form changed into a tall, barefooted young man, wearing a loincloth and holding a silver dagger.

Madame Caveat froze. She sneered then laughed. "Siding with humans, young prince?" she said. "This will surely mean war."

"You are a murderer, Caveat," replied the prince evenly. "We allowed you the wild things, but not the blood of fairies. You are banished from these lands."

Cackling, Madame Caveat folded her spider legs away beneath her shawls. "I will go. But you will rue the day you fought for humans."

Madame Caveat thrust a boney finger towards Tavin. "There lies your doom, noble prince. Kill him now; it may be your last chance."

With a howl of laughter, Madame Caveat jumped into the air and scuttled up a tree. She sang lustily, her evil song fading away into the brooding darkness.

Tavin felt a hand against his chest. The man in the dark coat tore the gag from his mouth. "Don't be afraid, dear boy. You're safe now."

Tavin coughed, his breath catching in pain. "Aria ..."

"She will be fine, Tavin. Everything is going to be okay."

Tavin frowned and rolled towards the voice. "How do you know my — ?"

He froze in shock.

Opa's soft blue eyes crinkled into a smile.

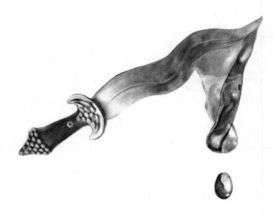

Blood Brothers

'Shick, shick, shick.'

Paper snowflakes.

He remembered making them with Moreanna, cutting little pieces out of folded paper and stringing the shapes up high in the windows.

'Shick, shick, shick.'

It was the sound that his mom's shearing scissors made as she cut fabric for Moreanna's dresses. Even as a little girl, Moreanna loved black lace and strange heavy fabrics that no department store ever stocked.

'Shick, shick, shick.'

His mom made Moreanna's dresses herself. Tavin remembered other women talking about those dresses, saying that it was inappropriate for a young girl to wear such dark colors. Tavin's mom made them anyways. She said that people had a right to be what they wanted. She said differences made the world beautiful.

Tavin opened his eyes slowly. He lay upon a narrow bed in a dark room filled with the smell of roasting meat. Red coals from an open stove cast enough light to make out the shapes that moved about him and murmured together in low voices.

Instinctively he reached out for Moreanna. She'd seemed so close in his dreams, but her presence fled as he woke.

A bolt of blue flashed across his vision at the foot of his bed. A dark shape knelt and stoked the fire, sending flames leaping. Tavin sucked in a sharp breath, recognizing Madame Caveat's cottage.

"There, that's better. Now we can move again." 'Shick, shick.' Aria sliced cleanly through the last strands of yarn entangling the room, and deftly collapsed the magical sword she held down to nothing.

"You are a very skilled bender." The second voice came from the figure kneeling by the coals. Tavin recognized his grandfather's voice.

Aria's white smile glimmered in the dimness. "I'm the only one I know who can build a sword from light," she said. "No one else has enough control for the edge."

"You are also the only female light mage I've ever met."

Aria's smile vanished. "That won't stop me from being the best," she said. "Nothing will."

Tavin's teeth knocked together. Despite the large fire, the chill still lingered in his bones.

The door to the cottage banged loudly. In strode a young man wearing nothing but a short loincloth and the silver-sheathed knife around his neck. His hair was fair and curly, his eyes set wide apart and black as coal. Tavin studied the young man for a long moment, suspicious of his easy movements. His eyes flickered towards Aria. She watched the newcomer as well, the fire bringing a bright rosy color to her cheeks.

Tavin struggled to sit up. He clutched his blankets to him as he moved. "Opa, what's going on?"

Opa, leaning upon his staff, pressed Tavin back down.

"Lay still, Tavin. I have fed you something to help warm you up, but it is not enough. You must stay calm until we can finish your healing."

Tavin's thoughts moved like cold porridge. "Why are we here? Caveat will be back, and who is he?"

Aria snorted. She bit a chunk off something she'd pulled from the fire with her knife, and licked her fingers with a show of great delight. "Not anytime soon," she said. "Prince Whelin banished her."

Tavin stared hard at the newcomer. He looked friendly enough, but Tavin wasn't sure he liked him.

"Where's your crown?" he asked.

Aria pinched Tavin on the toe. "Be respectful."

The young man smiled and dropped the load of firewood he carried. "Left it back at the palace — along with the rest of the useless junk they try and make a prince carry around."

"Like clothes?" Tavin returned drily.

Prince Whelin grinned. "More clothes make it harder to shape shift, besides — I never get cold."

Tavin looked over at Aria, still hungrily tearing into the meat she held with her sharp fangs. He frowned, recognizing the green collar Aria wore around her wrist. "Don't tell me you're eating her pet!"

Aria grinned devilishly. "It is only fair." She held out the knife. "Want some?"

"Tavin," Opa interrupted, "be careful not to get too excited. The gravechill is again building. We have to be ready."

Tavin looked hard at Opa. He didn't remember the exact moment he'd lost consciousness in the forest but he had the vague impression of movement and voices. He especially remembered the touch of his grandfather's hands through his jacket. The old man must have carried him.

A shiver began at the back of Tavin's neck and pressed its way down his spine. He became aware of the cold creeping deep into his chest.

"It would have taken you some time ago, if it weren't for Caveat," Opa said. "Oddly enough, when she roused you to fight she saved your life."

"She wanted to kill Aria," Tavin said. "I couldn't — "

Opa smiled. "She gave you a reason to live."

"What is it? What's wrong with me?"

"Gravechill affects those who have touched the nearly dead." Opa watched Tavin closely. "The spirits draw away the life of a living being to make themselves stronger."

"The nearly dead," Tavin repeated Opa's words. "Lucy, and Demetre. And ..." He couldn't finish his thought. He couldn't hear his sister, but he could feel her. He was sure he'd know if she died.

"Soon it will be time," Opa said. "The potion is wearing away and the sickness grows in strength."

The prince freed his dagger and placed the blade among the coals at the edge of the fire.

"The knife must be hot enough to break the ice and warm his blood." Opa passed his hand over Tavin's mouth feeling the chill of Tavin's breath.

"Tavin," Opa pulled a chair close. "Tavin, focus on my words. Don't let them go."

Tavin nodded, entranced by the ferocity in his grandfather's blue eyes.

"In the beginning" Opa said, "the world was one. The Starbreather made the earth and all the creatures upon it. The forces of creation, destruction, and magic were placed in perfect balance." Opa took a breath. "Magic was born from the Starbreather's song and dragons flew free upon wings of music, daring to climb even to the stars. Creation was built on dreams and hope. Destruction was nothing but the deep sleep of transformation, and no one feared it."

Tavin felt his mind grow hungry for Opa's words. They seemed to explain something he'd known for years but had never been able to express. Opa caught the yearning look in Tavin's eyes and smiled faintly.

"Magic," Opa said. "At its core, magic is the life-spark. It doesn't create or renew but it animates ..." Opa faltered. "Magic, balanced with creation, gives life — in a slow, orderly, and beautiful way. Magic on its own is wild and difficult to harness. The clans of Etheria are divided among those who wield magic and those who are born of it. Fairies are wielders," Opa nodded towards Aria, "their magic turns light itself into a living force — one that they can shape and manipulate. One day perhaps, you'll meet a Shamelin — a wild creature whose very essence is magic ..." Opa trailed off. "After building the world the Starbreather created thirteen races, including man, and told them to walk free upon the earth and shape it as they wished."

Opa shifted slightly. Tavin hung on his every word. Time seemed to slow.

"We were at peace," Opa continued. "Then Nod, an ancient one — a creature born of wild magic and one of the first created — desired to rule. She used her power to bend the force of destruction to her purpose, and entrapped the power of creation to remake the world as she wished."

"But it was too much for her. She couldn't contain the gathered forces of magic, creation, and destruction alone. There was a great explosion. The universe tore into four pieces: Alathia, where the golden servants of the Starbreather live forever; Golgotha, where fire burns and creatures devour one another; Earth, with little magic but rich in creation; and Earth's sister, Etheria, the seat of magic still."

Twelve of the original races remain in Etheria. The fracturing of worlds left Man on Earth, and for the most part, he has forgotten Etheria. Nod lives still, trapped behind a wall of fire in Golgotha."

Tavin shivered. "The Unmaker lives there, doesn't he?"

Opa caught his breath. "How do you know of him?"

Tavin tried to speak but a freezing wave of cold hit him, causing his teeth to chatter so violently he thought he might bite off his tongue.

"Whelin," Opa said. "We cannot delay longer!"

The prince knelt by the fire and slid his knife free from the coals. He didn't seem to notice the heat. He hesitated, his eyes blacker than the shadows. "If anyone ever finds out about this — "

"They will understand in the end," Opa replied. "Hurry."

Aria, who had grown very quiet, spoke up. "Whelin, what are you doing?"

The prince tightened his jaw. "Changing the world." He pulled back the blankets and sliced the red-hot dagger across Tavin's wrist. Tavin, too frozen to cry out from shock or to feel any pain, could only watch as his blood ran down his hand and began to pool upon the floor. He heard a rushing noise in his ears and felt suddenly weightless.

"Whelin!" Opa cried.

The prince turned the hot dagger upon himself. With a swift downward movement, he passed the blade over his own wrist. His blood sparkled like mercury, soft silver in color. Thick steaming drops ran to the ends of his fingertips.

The prince held his arm out and pressed their wrists together, clamping them tightly with his good hand.

Tavin felt a warm tingle in his hand and then down the length of his arm. The silver blood steamed as it fell on the floor, mingling with human blood. The prince's shoulders began to sag; dark circles formed beneath his eyes.

The warmth hit Tavin's chest. His heart lurched and began to beat like a bird fluttering in a cage. Tavin's eyes cleared and his tongue loosened. His arms and legs warmed, tingling painfully with pins and needles. He jerked upright and began to cough, feeling the warm air in the little cottage rush freely into his lungs.

The prince pulled back, slumping to the floor in exhaustion. Aria hissed through her teeth and ran to him. She knelt on the floor and caught the prince in her arms, glaring up at Tavin and Opa in a mixture of confusion, anger, and relief.

Tavin turned his wrist over, wiping away the mingled blood. The cut had already healed, leaving only the faintest of scars.

"What happened?"

"Never — not for a human," Aria stared at Tavin in awe.

"The royal blood of the Elche heals many things — when given freely," Opa said. "It is more precious than all the gold on earth."

Hope, like golden light, flooded Tavin's soul. "Please," he said, "give me some of your blood so I can cure my sister from her illness."

Aria hissed. "Fool," she snapped. "You don't deserve the gift he gave."

Tavin didn't care. "Please. I'll do anything."

The firelight cast the prince's nearly naked body into sharp relief. Color was rapidly returning to his cheeks. Only a scar, similar to Tavin's, marked the place where he'd cut his wrist.

"Tavin," Opa urged. "Your sister, she does not have the type of sickness you can cure with a potion. There is a darkness inside of her that is eating her soul."

"How do you know?" Tavin snapped.

"Because I was not the only one who wrote letters," Opa replied.

"You never said anything before."

Opa looked sad. "I'm sorry, Tavin, but I have no answer to give you. I have searched for months; I cannot find the source of Moreanna's darkness."

Tavin ground his teeth and turned back to the prince. "Please!"

Prince Whelin shook his head. "Even if I could help your sister, it will be some time before I am strong enough."

Aria barred her teeth. "You have no idea what he just did for you," she said. "The son of the Emperor just committed treason — and for what? A human!"

"Hush, Aria," the prince said. Leaning against the wall, he climbed slowly to his feet. "Klause. Show me the sign you spoke of."

With a solemn nod, Opa rolled up the sleeve on his right hand and turned up his palm. In the center of his palm was a white star-shaped scar. Opa looked at Tavin with a smile.

Tavin glowered back.

"I wanted to show you this the moment I saw you upon our doorstep with a worm in your pocket," Opa said. "I wished to tell you right away, but there is a proper time for everything." Opa gazed significantly at Tavin, as if measuring him up. "I am a human mage, a wielder of magic. Magic, when combined with the raw elements of creation, assumes one of its most powerful forms. I control the element of Earth."

Once again, Opa's mouth curled up into a secret smile.

"When I was seven," he said, "the Starbreather gave me the task of keeping the peace between our worlds. This is his mark. He named me a Guardian."

Tavin's mouth opened. "The Starbreather's alive?"

Opa nodded warmly. "Show them, Tavin."

Tavin locked his jaw, feeling as if someone had just dumped a bucket of cold water over his head. "So you meet some crazy person when you're a kid, what does that have to do with me?"

"You already know."

"It was an accident," Tavin said. "Just an old scar."

Opa placed a hand upon Tavin's arm. "Does it hurt more to hear a lie or to repeat it, Tavin? Show them."

A muscle flexed in Tavin's neck. "I'd rather not."

Opa frowned. "Tavin—Whelin saved your life. It is a small thing."

"Fine," Tavin snarled. "It's not like it means anything anyways." He stood, shrugged out of his jacket and yanked his shirt over his head. "Happy?"

His scar tore its way across his chest, carving its wide mark deep into the muscle. The skin around it was puckered and red. The scar itself was pale, almost white, and shaped like a star.

The prince nodded slowly. "Now I understand," he said.

Tavin's cheeks flushed angrily. "Don't say anything, okay? I hate it when people look at me like that. I have enough problems already." He turned towards Opa. "This thing has made me a freak. I don't care if you think it's some kind of magical branding. Every day I have to face the memories it brings. Even if I wanted to forget, I can't."

Tavin clenched his teeth. "If these are the kind of gifts your Starbreather gives," he said, "I don't want anything to do with him."

Opa leaned heavily on his staff. "You have been chosen, Tavin. You are also called as a Guardian."

"What kind of dumb job is that?" Tavin snapped. "Why in the world would I risk my neck to protect this place? In case you haven't noticed, everyone hates us!"

"Tavin …" Aria rose to her feet. She couldn't take her eyes off the scar. "It's beautiful," she whispered.

Tavin ignored her. "I never asked to be part of this," he said.

"Does a bird ask to fly?" Opa tried a smile.

Tavin clenched his fists. "Where were you when I needed you? Where were you when my mother died, or when my father left?" he said. "I don't owe you anything."

"This changes everything," Aria said. She moved towards Tavin, as if drawn towards his scar.

Tavin flashed her an angry look. "It changes nothing."

The prince dropped a hand upon Aria's shoulder. "Aria, come. I will take you home."

"No."

The prince looked confused. "What do you mean?"

"I'm not going home." Aria turned to stand near Tavin. He shivered as her hand brushed the scar on his chest. "They want to take my magic, and this human has sworn to give me sanctuary."

"This is not wise. If you wish, you may come with me; we will speak of it to my father."

"It's my choice." Aria stuck out her chin, her eyes flashing. "You don't know what it's like."

The prince looked as if he wanted to say more, but changed his mind. "So be it," he said. The air about him shimmered with light. He dropped forward towards the ground and grew in size. When the light dimmed, a tall stag with a crown of ebony antlers tangling among the rafters stood before them. He seemed to take up the whole cottage. Opa bowed his head; Aria turned her eyes towards the floor, her cheeks bright pink.

Tavin's mouth fell slack. Like the others, he was unable to look away. He couldn't deny the magnificence of the creature before him. Every part of the stag seemed to radiate courage and justice. Rather than inspire confidence, however, Tavin felt something small and ugly slide into place deep in his heart. He slid his eyes sideways, trying to read Aria's expression.

"I will stay to burn this cottage to the ground," said the prince. "You must flee before anyone discovers humans were here."

Opa caught Tavin's hand and began moving him towards the cottage door. "Thank you, Whelin," Opa said. "Thank you for saving my grandson's life. We honor the treaty and the kindness of your family."

"Be careful, Klause," the Prince Whelin said. "If it becomes known that a fully trained human mage walked freely in our world, I'm not sure even the royal family could protect you."

"Why does everyone hate us?" Tavin asked. "What did we do to them?"

Prince Whelin's coal black eyes clouded over. "Has no one told you?"

Tavin frowned. "Told me what?"

Prince Whelin looked down at him with sympathy. His voice grew somber. "Queen Nod's most loyal and terrible servant, the Unmaker, was a human."

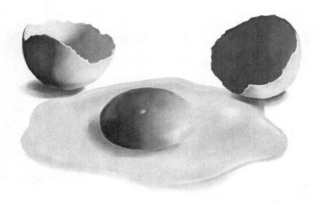

Chickens And Chores

Tavin awoke the next morning on the floor of his bedroom with the brush of whiskers tickling his nose. He sneezed and groaned sleepily. The morning sun shone in his eyes. Cold air whispered over his blanket through the open balcony door. His whole body felt sore and bruised.

Pip, looking alarmed, slowly poked his nose past the clothing pile where he'd hidden. He bounded out and scolded Tavin in rat chatter.

"You're the scavenger," Tavin whispered. "Why don't you get

breakfast for a change? Now scoot! You'll wake her."

Tavin rolled over, pushed back the tangle of blankets and stretched. Pip, seeing he'd have to work for breakfast, snapped his teeth in a huff and captured one of Tavin's socks, dragging it into the abyss beneath Tavin's bed.

Tavin ran his fingers through his hair and yawned, trying to catch his waking thoughts. He couldn't help but watch the bed where she lay. He could make out the curve of her shoulder beneath the blankets. Her dark red hair spread across the white pillow in curling inky rivers.

Tavin's fingers brushed across his bare chest and he jerked them back as if scalded.

"Hey, you." Aria turned and blinked sleepily down at him from his bed. She looked like a small animal peering out of a cave of blankets. Her hair was a glorious mess. Her eyes looked dark as pine trees.

Tavin nervously pulled the covers around his shoulders. "Hey," he said, his voice croaking. "Sorry if I woke you. How'd you sleep?"

Aria smiled like a cherry blossom and tumbled out of bed, pulling the blankets with her. "Let me see it," she said.

Tavin flinched.

"You don't have to hide from me."

"Girls always hate it," he said. "They say it's disgusting."

"I'm not like human girls." Aria smirked mischievously and walked her fingers up his arm. "But you already know that."

Tavin let out a slow breath and lowered the blanket.

Aria propped herself up on one elbow and pressed her hand

against the middle of Tavin's scar. Blue sparks crackled and leapt from the ends of her fingertips, giving Tavin a jolt. He pulled back in surprise.

"Does it hurt?" she asked.

Tavin shook his head. "No. No, I was just startled. I didn't expect that."

Aria bit her lip. "No one's trained you and the magic is already waking. I've heard of the mark Guardians wear," she said. "But I've never seen one."

Tavin crossed his arms. "I'm not a Guardian."

"Tavin, you've been blessed. This means you can do amazing things."

"That's not how I read it."

"It's a perfect star. It's His mark." She reached forward again.

Tavin stood and tugged a shirt over his head. "Look, I'm glad you get to start over and everything, but I'm leaving."

Aria frowned. "When?"

"Tomorrow, hopefully. My sister needs me home. There's no cure for her here."

"You meant it, didn't you?" she said. She gnawed on the corner of her thumbnail. "What you said about not trusting the Starbreather?"

"Yeah … I did."

Aria stood. The tee shirt she'd borrowed left most of her legs bare. She stepped near, drawing herself tall. "You're really leaving me."

"Well, I'm not — ," Tavin hesitated, his palms suddenly damp. "I mean, maybe I can visit if you'd like."

Aria pressed a finger against his lips. "I wonder what my father would say if he found out I'd kissed a human?"

Tavin's breath caught in his throat, his mind spinning in several crazy directions at once. "I — um … well, I don't think he'd be happy about it."

Aria smiled and slid her body, panther-like, against his. "You have no idea."

Tavin stood very still, not sure what to make of this new Aria, yet afraid to frighten her off.

She chuckled. "You can't understand. There are some from my world who would kill us for even being in the same room."

Tavin pulled back. "You're serious, aren't you?"

Aria wrapped her hand around the back of his head and drew him close again. Her eyes pinned him to the spot. "Very serious."

A loud knock on the bedroom door nearly caused Tavin to swallow his tongue.

"Tavin? … Tavin? I know you are there!"

Tavin hissed through his teeth and pressed a hand over Aria's mouth to stifle her giggles.

The doorknob jiggled. "Why do you lock your door?" Oma's voice was sharp and pestering. "I wish to see you!"

"One moment!" Tavin turned towards Aria, pushing her towards the wardrobe. "Quick!" he said. "It's my Oma, you've got to hide!"

Aria, biting her lip so hard her eyes watered, climbed inside.

"I'm getting dressed, Oma!" Tavin tucked Aria behind a long jacket and shut the wardrobe, leaving only the smallest crack.

"We'll talk about this later," he said in a hoarse whisper.

Tavin reached for the door.

Oma swept into the room like an avenging queen; her hair tottering in a bun, her chin high, and her half-moon spectacles perched on the very end of her long pointy nose.

"Jeez! Give a guy some warning will you?"

Oma Nadia's cheeks flushed with rosy temper. "Where did you go? You left with no note, nothing!"

"I — I went to see a friend in town."

"You are just like an American!" Oma declared. "You eat our food, you come and go as you please, and you do no work! You do not think about how my poor hands ache and my feet swell. All you think is for yourself!"

"I'm not your slave." Tavin snapped. "I don't have to do anything."

Oma's mouth pressed into a thin line.

"Besides," Tavin continued, trying to sound reasonable again, "I'm leaving tomorrow."

"If you leave you will be like your father; we will never see you again," Oma said.

Tavin hadn't expected her to say that.

She turned her face away. "Everyone leaves, what does it matter? I expect nothing less."

Tavin took one of Oma's hands, feeling a twinge of sympathy. He knew all too well what it felt like to be abandoned. The bones in her hands felt like dry twigs. "I'm not him, Oma. I'm not going to disappear."

Oma pulled her hand away. When she looked at him again, her face had lost its weakness.

"What did you do to make such a mess?" she said. "Do I not have enough work to do?"

Oma shoved a finger towards a damp trail of grave dirt and mud staining the hallway, marking a grimy path towards the shower. Her foot began tapping. Tavin scrambled to come up with a believable excuse. Before he could, however, Oma threw her hands into the air and snorted through her nose.

"Why do I care if you run away at night and fall into a ditch? You are a city boy. You do what you like!"

"It was an accident," Tavin said. "Go drink some tea or something. I'll clean it up, okay?"

Oma took a breath. "Today you will help Opa with his chores. He is very tired and you are a strong boy."

Tavin hesitated, thinking of Aria. "I'll go in a minute."

Oma's gaze flickered dangerously. "If you wish to eat you must work. Klause will teach you." She turned and strode from the room.

Tavin gritted his teeth, pulled on his sneakers, and headed for the barn. As he entered the courtyard, he looked over his shoulder and saw Oma's pale face peering at him through the kitchen window. He shook his head in frustration. He hoped Aria had enough sense to stay hidden.

The sun lanced brightly through the eaves of the old stone and wood barn. Inside, the smell of hay, manure, and animals was nearly overwhelming. The heat given off by the animals would be stifling by the afternoon.

Tavin, his eyes watering, found Opa near the back. "Oma said I should help you."

Opa, breathing heavily, stopped and leaned on his pitchfork. His eyes twinkled.

"My Nadia is a fireball. Your father had her temper. I think perhaps you have it too?"

Tavin shrugged, but Opa just chuckled. "There is a shovel against the wall and a pair of boots. Bring the wheelbarrow. How is the fairy?"

"Her name's Aria. She's hanging out in my room."

"Be careful, Tavin. Fairies rarely do anything for anyone but themselves."

"They don't like you either, remember?" Tavin dropped the wheelbarrow by Opa. "Oma doesn't know, does she?"

Opa tossed soiled hay into the wheelbarrow. "She would not approve."

"What do you think about it all?" asked Tavin. "I mean the Starbreather and everything. It's all just so crazy!"

"There," Opa pointed. "Use the shovel to clean the cow dung, I will sift the hay."

Tavin grabbed the shovel.

"Becoming a Guardian is a gift, a wonderful gift," Opa said. "You do not need to fear it."

Tavin remained quiet as he began working. "Why do you do it?" he asked finally.

"Because, while I do not trust fairies or goblins, I still love them," Opa replied.

"They'd kill you if they could," Tavin said.

Opa grinned warily. "They could try."

Tavin wrinkled his nose as he lifted the cow patties. Despite the work, his heart felt lighter. There was something wholesome about the feel of a shovel in his hands.

"It takes work," Opa said.

"What?" Tavin grunted and levered an extra large load into the wheelbarrow.

"Mastering your power."

"I told you. I don't want it."

Opa paused and mopped his forehead. "Our family has lived on this land four hundred years. Did you know this village used to stand on the edge of a swamp? For many generations the swamp choked the fields with mud and poisonous plants. The rain only made it worse. Nothing could be planted here, all year around.

When our family came, we gathered the village and worked together to build canals. The swamp drained and the poisonous plants withered. After some years, the swamp was gone and in its place there was very rich earth. Our village planted crops and fed many towns. What was once a curse became a blessing."

Tavin locked his jaw, working on in silence.

"Do you understand me?" Opa asked.

"I get it."

"Tavin," Opa pressed. "You must not miss this. It is about our family. Even before the mark was given to us, we were providers and protectors. The village prospered because of us."

"It's not doing so well these days, is it?"

"These days are dark days. Once the Gates between our two worlds were open and everyone traveled freely, and then — "

"The Unmaker came."

"He brought war and a curse upon our land." Opa looked hard into Tavin's eyes. "It was a human hand that caused the bonds of friendship between our lands to break. A human hand must now bring healing."

Opa left the barn and returned with buckets and a hose. Together they rinsed the concrete floor of the stall with water and swept it dry with straw brooms. Steam rose up through the sunlight and danced against the walls.

"Tell me about your power," Tavin said.

Opa nodded. "There are four types of human mages: Earth, Wind, Water, and Fire mages. You must study each element and choose one."

"What happens when you choose an element?" Tavin asked.

"When you are ready, you release it. Then the power of the other elements fades, giving you more control over the one."

"How long does all that take?"

"If you are a good student — if you work hard and listen carefully — you may begin to use your element in five or six months."

"Sounds like a lot of work."

Opa peered at Tavin thoughtfully. "It is a grave and wonderful journey," he said. "Such a gift would be worth less if it cost nothing." Opa looked at Tavin with a long measuring gaze. He was solemn and proud, like the king of a besieged kingdom.

They took a break, enjoying the sunshine in the garden.

"Did you ever do this with Dad?" Tavin asked.

"Yes, many times. Your father liked to work."

"He's never talked about this place."

"It was difficult for us when he left. It was not what we would have wished."

"What happened?"

Opa smiled.

"Your mother loved the city. We would have him stay, so we could teach our grandchildren, but your father did not listen and he left with her. After your mother died, when all the magic in the world could not bring her back, he refused to teach you and Moreanna about your birthright."

They returned to the barn, laying fresh straw for the cows.

"Did you ever look for Dad?" Tavin asked. "After he crossed over?"

Opa gazed over the garden wall and into the fields beyond. "He should not have gone. It was a fool's errand. He thinks he can find your mother in one of the beyond places."

"What are those?"

"More worlds," Opa replied vaguely. "They are not for living mortals."

"But you looked for him?"

Opa sighed. "Yes, for a little while. Then I turned back."

"Why? He's your son!"

Opa hung his pitchfork on a peg. "A Guardian is responsible for many lives. The life of one person is not worth the risk of starting another war: not yours, mine, or even your father's. I could not travel far in the Shadowlands without being discovered. As it is, I have broken many rules. If he is able, your father must return on his own."

"I'd never give up on my son like that." Tavin retorted. "I know what it's like to be left behind. I wouldn't wish it on my worst enemy."

"Tavin, you must not break the peace."

Tavin tightened his jaw. "For Moreanna, I'll do anything."

Opa's face was grey and heavy. "It has been a long morning," he said. "I must take a rest."

"What's left to do?"

Opa motioned towards the cages where chickens clucked bossily to one another. "I have not yet gathered the eggs or cleaned the cages."

"Don't bother," Tavin said. "I'll finish."

Opa nodded and left, his shoulders bowed. Tavin watched him, feeling a twinge of guilt, but not able to regret any of his words. He blew out his cheeks and turned towards the chicken coops.

As it turned out, it wasn't the gathering or the cleaning that was the problem. It was the chicken catching.

They seemed to take it personally. Every time Tavin opened the wire door to a cage, chickens screeched and nipped at his fingers. More often than not, after a flurry of wings and a fruitless struggle,

Tavin found himself with smashed egg in one hand, straw in his hair, and a chicken ruffling its feathers as it ran free in the barn.

One chicken vanished behind the stacks of hay piled against the back wall. Tavin edged up as close to the crack as possible, reaching his arm down. "Here chicky, chicky ... here chicky, chicky."

He felt the soft touch of feathers, then a sharp pinch. Tavin yelped and stuck his bleeding finger in his mouth.

"You sure have a way with animals."

Tavin jumped, looking up for the voice.

Perched high in the rafters sat Aria. She wore a dress the color of the sky and white leggings. Her wild hair was pulled neatly back into a braid. Tavin almost would have said she looked dressed up if it weren't for her heavy boots, a woolly scarf, and the pair of goggles pushed up on her forehead.

She grinned and jumped lightly to the ground.

"I, uh, never got along with chickens," he said. "I like dogs better."

"Rats too," she said. "There is a nest under your bed." She crossed her arms. "Don't look at me like that. I fed him breakfast."

Tavin bit back a smile. "I call him Pip. I've known him two days and he's already a master beggar."

"Do you always make friends with rats?"

"Well, yeah ... and other things. You know ... the animals everyone else hates. I figure someone should give them a chance."

"Defender of the ugly," Aria said.

Tavin felt his cheeks grow hot. "What of it?"

Aria shook her head. "It's admirable." She crouched down and made a low clicking noise in her throat. A moment later, the chicken poked its head around a bale and fluttered happily into her waiting arms. She handed the bird to Tavin.

Tavin, remembering the touch of her skin, felt his heart speed up.

She wrinkled her nose as if she'd read his thoughts.

"Wash up first," she said. "You smell worse than usual. When you are finished, meet me in the fields at the big tree. I have a surprise for you."

Open Skies

Half an hour later, Tavin followed a dirt road over the yellow rolling hills, heading for the tree Aria had mentioned. Teilenheim Village vanished from view, tucked into a hidden valley. Tavin stopped to catch his breath.

He felt the light brush of Moreanna's mind as if in welcome. His heart flooded with warmth. The faint image of a pale, dark-eyed girl appeared beside him, rippling in the air.

Moreanna!

Tavin. She looked sad.

Where have you been? he asked. *I've missed you. I have so much to tell you!*

Moreanna bowed her head.

I'm not what I was, she said. *You need to come home.*

I will.

Good.

The image wavered and blew away. A moment later, she was gone again.

Even the smell of sun-baked earth couldn't drive out the chill that settled over Tavin's heart. His steps grew heavy.

"The fairy's using you."

The voice came from close behind him. Tavin spun around in surprise. Demetre strolled towards him through wavering stalks of canola, his face sour and pointy. "I thought we were friends," he said, "but you've invited the enemy into your bedroom."

"She's not the enemy," Tavin said. "She's been helping the whole time."

Demetre sucked in his cheeks. "I also thought you could read people. That little fairy has you wrapped around her finger. What has she helped with? Finding your father? A cure for your sister's illness?"

"Leave me alone," Tavin said.

"That headache you have," Demetre said, "that fogginess in your brain like you can't tell which side is up anymore, that's her; she's done something to you. If your gift was working properly you'd know that."

Tavin spun angrily. "I said leave me alone!"

"What about the prince? What have you got to offer her next to someone like him?"

"I don't care about what you think you know." Tavin formed a fist. "She cares about me. Whoever locked you away did both our worlds a favor."

Demetre barred his teeth, looking like a small rodent. He jumped forward, his black eyes hard, and plunged his hands into Tavin's ribcage.

Tavin gasped as Demetre's ghostly hands gripped his heart.

"Maybe this will help you remember," Demetre said, hissing. "This is what death feels like. It is not the end, as you believe it to be, it is only a beginning: a thousand years of cold agony. Alone, always alone … remember this feeling well. When you are betrayed and locked in an icy cell of your own dying flesh, remember that I warned you."

Demetre vanished.

Tavin doubled over, falling to his knees. He coughed and shook, waiting until the sun warmed him and drove away Demetre's icy touch. He climbed slowly back to his feet. Farther down the road, on top of a round little hill, grassy and fallow, he saw a single spreading tree.

Tavin climbed the hill and settled down against the tree trunk. He pulled an apple from his pocket and took a big bite. Not every creature on the other side was evil. Good and bad were all mixed up in the Shadowlands, just the same way they were on Earth.

You had to take one with the other.

He took a few more bites of the apple, thoughts of death growing more distant as he ate. Something was wrong with Demetre, he decided. He'd been twisted somehow; he could no longer see the good in people.

A loud thump interrupted his thoughts. He jerked back in surprise and banged his head against the tree.

With a falling laugh, Aria dropped out of the sky. Her blue wings, once again mended, spread behind her like angel's wings. Her red hair shone like phoenix feathers in the sun.

Tavin scrambled to his feet. "Give a guy some warning will you?" he scolded, rubbing his head. "I'm not used to having fairies tumbling out of the sky!"

Aria knotted her arms around his neck. "You look pale," she said. "Are you feeling okay?"

"I'm fine."

"Are you sure?"

Tavin pushed her back and tossed away his apple core. "Yes."

"Then it's good to see you too. Are you ready?"

"For what?"

Aria tapped him on the nose with a slender finger. "A gift. Now, close your eyes. Good … open them again." She held out a pair of goggles, made with leather and heavy glass lenses. "I found these in your grandfather's attic."

"Wow, just what I always wanted — " Tavin rolled his eyes playfully. "How did you know?"

Aria smirked. With a flourish, she pulled out a second pair of wings from behind her back. They were much larger than the first pair and glimmered with deep hues of orange. Tavin's breath caught in his throat.

"Someone told me once that humans dream of flying," Aria said. "The first time I came to your world I hid a spool of fairy silk in the garden. I made these last night while you slept."

"What do I do?" Tavin stumbled over his words in his eagerness to touch the wings.

With a laugh, Aria held out the wings and showed Tavin the two nearly invisible loops for him to slip his arms through. They fit snugly across his back and as they settled into place, he felt a light tingling followed by the sensation of slight pressure between his shoulder blades.

"I can't believe this!" Tavin looked down, startled to realize he'd risen a foot from the ground.

"Be careful," Aria said. "You'll get tangled up in the tree! You must relax!"

Tavin tried to focus. The wings moved like an extension of his body, as if he'd gained a new muscle group. He willed his wings to slow and drifted back towards the ground.

"Flying up and down is easy," Aria said. She handed him the goggles. "It's the wind that's troublesome. You can fly against it but you will tire quickly. The best is to launch into a friendly air current and ride it to another. Here, I'll show you."

Aria walked a few steps away from the tree. Pulling her goggles down she turned her face towards the sky and waited.

Her body tensed like a surfer waiting to catch a wave.

On cue, Aria sprinted a couple steps and jumped into the air. Immediately she picked up speed and shot upwards into the blue sky.

Tavin watched as the fairy moved expertly from one current to another, sometimes closing her wings and dropping a short ways before being caught again by the wind and spinning gracefully in another direction.

After a few more turns Aria dropped down, neatly landing a few steps from Tavin.

"Do all fairies fly like that?" Tavin was seriously impressed.

Aria grinned in pleasure. "Most don't bother. Flying is just transportation. They don't like the wind — they wait for calm days to get around."

"But that seems like the best part!"

Aria's green eyes sparkled. "I agree. There's nothing better than the wind at your back."

Tavin moved away from the tree. He buttoned his jacket closed and pulled his goggles over his eyes.

"Here it comes!" Aria grabbed his hand. They jumped together. Tavin yelled with joy. The warm current carried them quickly up and over the tree. The wide fields dropped and spun in circles beneath him.

Tavin steadied himself, then let go of Aria's hand. He immediately flipped head over heels. She caught a hold of his ankle and tugged him right side up again. With laughter on her face, she showed Tavin how to stay upright by opening his arms wide. Then he looked down and his stomach leapt into his throat. The village had turned into a shadowy blob surrounded by bright squares of barley and canola.

In an instant Aria's hand was holding his. She gave his fingers a squeeze and Tavin blushed. He let go again, determined to do it on his own.

This time he stayed upright. After a few more tries, he learned to use his arms to angle his body in line with the current. The feeling of air rushing over and around him was the most glorious thing he'd ever felt in his life. This was nothing like the wild piggyback ride of before.

"Hey! Catch this one!" Aria said.

Tavin felt a slight drop in temperature. He realized they hovered on the edge of a cold slipstream. With a holler, Aria dove headfirst into the falling current. Tavin, afraid he'd chicken out, didn't give himself a chance to think and followed close behind.

He fell so fast he lost his breath. The ground filled his vision with a roar. Somewhere below him and to his right, Aria whooped and laughed in wild delight.

"Spread your wings, Tavin!" she said.

Gritting his teeth, Tavin popped his wings open. Below him, Aria did a graceful summersault and jumped to her right. Tavin copied her movement the best he could and tumbled into a warm updraft.

Aria drifted lazily towards the sun, her red hair loose and floating around her shoulders. Tavin flew up to her. Once they were level, he slowed down and hung easily at her side.

"Is it always like this?" he asked.

Aria smiled like a cat in the sun. "There are often storms on our side and the wind can be dangerous. On other days, there is no wind and staying in the air takes a lot of work. Although ... if you get high enough there's always a current. But no — today is special. Today is perfect for flying." Aria looked at Tavin from the corner of her eye. "I wanted you to know what it feels like."

Tavin released a breath. He looked down at the ground in its patchwork colors of green and yellow far beneath his feet. He felt giddy. "I couldn't even begin to explain what this is like!" he blurted. "I guess fairies take flying for granted. But you were right; this is the kind of thing humans only dream of."

Aria's eyes were bright. With a flash of rainbow wings, she flew a little higher. "Come on," she said. "There's something else I want to show you."

Weaving from one air current to another, Aria led Tavin towards a low green mountain. It reminded Tavin of a sleeping dragon. Dark fir trees rippled down its bulky sides and deep crevices winked up at him like watchful eyes. The late afternoon sun painted the base of the mountain in stripes of gold and deep purple. Near the peak, Tavin noticed a broken grassy bluff like a bald spot.

Aria changed directions; circling downwards towards the clearing. "There's a bit of a bump here," she said.

A cool pocket of air sucked Tavin forward, causing him to drop abruptly. He threw his weight backwards and pulled out of a sharp nosedive just in time to tumble to the ground.

Aria landed gracefully beside him.

"Cheer up!" she said. "Landing is always the hardest part."

Tavin groaned, feeling new bruises spread up his leg. Aria simply laughed, tugging him to his feet.

Thick with tall grass, brambles, and wildflowers, the bluff slanted downwards, halting abruptly at the edge of a high, rocky precipice. A crumbling wall, likely the ruins of a castle, leaned away from the rim of the cliff.

Birds, hidden within the ruins, called sweetly to the forest. Tavin grinned. He'd always loved old things. The castle ruins were secret and untouched. He wondered if a maze of passageways tunneled beneath his feet. He imagined a dragon's hold of treasure hidden close by.

"Can you see it?" asked Aria.

"What?"

"The Gate," she replied. "Do you see the Gate?"

Tavin looked again. He gave a long low whistle. "No way," he said. "Now that's a little scary."

A narrow arch in the wall, at the very edge of the precipice, opened into empty space. Tavin walked over for a closer look. Strange symbols were etched into the weathered keystone.

Tavin ran his fingers across the ancient stonework, watching in wonder as the symbols glimmered blue.

"No one really knows about this one," Aria said. "The secret's well guarded, since humans and about half of the creatures in Etheria don't fly. This meadow is my sanctuary."

"Where does the Gate go?"

"Well," replied Aria. "There's quite a drop. But it's close to where my family lives."

Tavin looked at her strangely. "I'm guessing I shouldn't know about this then."

Aria shrugged. "I told you, no one knows. It's my secret. Come on." She took hold of his hand and flew to the top of the ruin. It was warm and lazy up high, and they were able to find comfortable seats among the grass growing over the crumbled stone.

"I come here to get away," Aria said. She stretched out and tilted her head towards the sky. "Your world is so much warmer than ours. Ours feels so cold all the time. The sun on our side doesn't give half as much light."

"Why is it so different in the Shadowlands?" Tavin asked.

Aria chewed a nail. "When the Great Fracture happened, our side got most of the magic. Your side got creation."

"What do you mean?"

Aria spread her arms wide. "Look around you. Every morning makes this world new again. Trees and flowers bloom; babies are born every day." Aria reached a hand out and ran her fingers across the tops of a clover patch.

"We're dying," she said. "We have magic but little creation. We can't stop the sun from cooling. New flowers are rare. The last child was born a century ago."

Tavin frowned. "You're a hundred years old?"

Aria smiled crookedly. She held up two fingers.

"Two hundred?"

"Two hundred and thirteen. Soon I will be ready to join with another."

"You mean marriage?"

Aria nodded. She giggled. "It must be strange for you, but I've been a child for a long time. I'm ready to love now."

Tavin turned bright red. "I can't figure you out," he said at last. "I usually read people pretty well, but I never know what you're going to do or say next."

Aria's hand wandered up his side and across his chest. "I will try to be more clear," she said.

Tavin grabbed her hand. "I think before we hang out any more, I'd better let you know I'm only almost sixteen. I don't know what they think about it in your world, but in my world that makes us being together illegal."

Aria laughed. "Trust me," she said. "It's worse that you're human."

"Why?"

Aria grew quiet. She rolled over onto her side. "It's not just the Unmaker," she said at last. "He made things worse, but I think we wanted an excuse to hate humans."

"What's so wrong with us?"

"The reason is easy to see." Aria twisted her fingers through the long grass. "You've been to our world. Everything is rotten, dying. We are supposed to be the better side of the universe. We can make things of great beauty and we wield more power than most humans dream of … but it's all ending. One day we'll be gone. Our long lives will end and just like that—all of our secrets and magic will disappear. Etheria will be nothing but dead rock. And humans won't even notice." She fell back and squeezed her eyes shut. "You won't even ask the question."

Tavin reached for her hand, then stopped. She lay before him like a china doll; almost too finely built to be real. For the first time he realized that despite her strength, she was perilously fragile. He studied her hungrily, memorizing her form like a waking man grasping the details of a dream.

She opened her eyes. "We are lost. Soon our world will die. The Unmaker has already won. He doesn't even have to come back."

"He won't win."

She turned to him. "How do you know?"

"I told you — I know things. It's just this sense that I have."

Aria grinned slyly. "So you know what I'm thinking?"

"Um, well … no. I told you, when it comes to you I get confused." Tavin tried hard not to think of Demetre's words.

Aria laughed, causing Tavin to blush.

"I never understood it before," he said. "Morry has sort of the same thing, only stronger. I think it might be wrapped up with what Opa calls 'being a Guardian.'"

Aria pressed a finger to his chest. "A protector."

Tavin turned his face away. "I'm worried about my sister. I thought I still had time, but now I'm not so sure."

Aria propped herself up on one elbow. "Tell me what happened to you; why you won't trust the Starbreather."

Tavin cleared his throat. He met her eyes then looked away.

"I don't like talking about it."

Aria didn't move. "Tell me," she repeated.

Tavin reached into his pocket for a rubber band. "It happened when I was eight," he said. "One night, after mom tucked me in and gave me a hug ... I don't know, maybe I made that part up ... a fire started in my parent's bedroom." Tavin frowned and pinched his forehead. He didn't know how he was supposed to say it.

Aria found his hand.

"My dad ran to our room and dragged Morry and I out," he continued. "It was only after we were safe that he realized my mom hadn't come with him. He just stood there, holding our hands, watching our house blaze and wondering why she didn't come out." Tavin rubbed his eyes. They burned, yet the tears wouldn't come. He'd finished crying a long time ago. "I pulled free," Tavin said, "and ran back into the house before he could stop me. My dad wouldn't go back for her — so I went myself. I made it as far as the living room. I saw her through the flames, right before a beam from the roof fell in and pinned me to the floor ... that's where this came from." Tavin struck his chest. "I heard my mom screaming." Tavin clenched his teeth. "My sister told the fire fighters where to find me, but by the time they had come, mom was already dead."

Tavin took a deep breath. "My dad ... he should have been the one going back into the house, not me. I wasn't strong enough, but he could have saved her. Later, I guess he thought he could bring my mother back. At least that's what Opa said. Dad left two years ago, but he really left when she died — when we needed him the most.

Morry and I have been orphans ever since that day."

"Tavin ..." Aria's eyes filled with tears.

Tavin pulled back. "If my mother burning to death while I watched was part of some cosmic plan, I don't want to hear about it."

"What if it's not that simple?" Aria asked.

"Don't. And don't you dare look at me like that."

"Like what?"

"Like, 'you're so sorry I've had such a bad life.' I'm sick of people being sorry for me. Trust me, I know: there's nothing you can say to make it right. I've heard it all."

She kissed him.

It was wet, and long. It took Tavin's breath away. She drew him against her and lay back upon the grass. Sparks arced from her fingers, sending a dull buzz through his chest. When they finally parted, Tavin's mind was on fire.

Aria closed her eyes, a smile on her soft lips. "Hush." She reached up, her fingers caressing his face. She tilted her chin back and gazed at the sky. "I can't bring your mother back," she said finally, "and I can't speak for the one who marked you, but maybe there is something I can do to help."

"What? Do you know a way to cure my sister?" Tavin wanted to kiss her again. His body ached for it.

Aria sat up. "My people have a book," she said. "It is one of our greatest secrets. In it are detailed records of all known magic in Etheria. Every spell and how it works. Only fairies training to become mages are allowed to read it. It heals, it enchants. Just looking at it can do things to you …" Aria shifted so she could gaze deep into Tavin's eyes.

"Help me get it," she said. "And you'll have enough magic to raise your sister from dead."

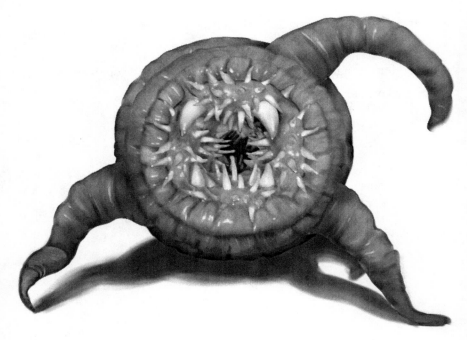

Grubark

avin looked down. He passed over fields and trees so fast his cheeks burned with cold and his goggles fogged with tears. Aria flew ahead of him, a dull blue streak against the pale sky. Next to her quick precise movements, he flew like a fat seagull.

Tavin took a fast look over his shoulder. The cliff Gate, hung like a doorway in space, blurred into the horizon. He caught one last glimpse of the bright meadow they'd left behind before it winked out of sight.

He hoped Aria had a plan; his last visit to the Shadowlands had brought him no closer to finding a cure, and had nearly killed him in the process. He squinted up at the sky. Despite the clearness of the day, the sun looked dull and old.

Aria banked sharply, dropping into a steep dive towards a wet-looking patch of land. Tavin tried to follow and plummeted like a stone into a deep air pocket. He lurched forward, searching for a gentler current, and hit the black swamp face-first.

He couldn't tell which way was up or down. In every direction, there was nothing but murky water. Slimy weeds wrapped about his wrists and ankles. He made a powerful thrust with his wings and tore free.

Choking and spitting, he broke the surface. Slick trees with black trunks grew out of the swamp. They were lifted from the water on stiff vertical roots. Branches, covered in slimy grey moss, dragged across the mire. Above, the sun struggled to penetrate a high roof of thick rubbery leaves.

Tavin struggled to land. The sand sank beneath his every step, re-minding him of bad dreams running from monsters. His bedraggled wings trailed limply behind him. Aria, standing serenely on the spot where she'd landed, looked at him and burst out laughing.

"Here," she said. "Those things aren't good any anymore. Let me help you."

She took hold of the straps that held on his wings and tugged them up over his head. She shook the wings like bed sheets, flicking off the worst of the mud. "They'll fly again," she said. "Once they're clean and dry. But I'm afraid they'll never be the same."

She looked up at his face and laughed again, clutching her side. "I'm sorry," she said, wiping her eyes. "But that's got to be the worst landing I've ever seen."

Tavin mischievously slid an arm around the small of her back, slicking her clothes with mud. He pressed close, hoping for another kiss. "Can I have this dance?"

"Yuck!" Aria knocked him to the ground.

Tavin lobbed a handful of mud at her. Aria dodged and pulled a blue sword out of the air.

"That is so awesome," Tavin said. "How do — "

The sword plunged forward, pricking his throat.

"Gotcha," she said.

Tavin tried a laugh. "Looks like it."

Aria smiled oddly and flicked her wrist. The sword vanished.

Tavin climbed to his feet, his hands cold. There had been something in her eyes — just for a moment.

"You sure you're not crazy?" he asked.

Aria tossed her head.

"All boys need to know their place," she said.

"What does that even mean?" he asked.

Aria shrugged. Then her eyes widened; her gaze on the black swamp behind him. "Forget it, we've got bigger problems."

A low creaking groan, like the bending of cedars in the wind, sounded through the swamp. The ground trembled and the water swelled.

Tavin turned, searching in his pockets for a weapon. He found his pocketknife.

In the middle of the swamp, something — bigger than a transport truck and shaped roughly like a slug — rose slowly from the mire.

With a heave that drowned the shore, the oily mound reared above them. A round mouth, with rows of jagged teeth that could mulch a tree, slid open beneath folds of rotting and wrinkled flesh.

The thing began to speak, its teeth grinding together like gears on a truck.

"What a story runs through the water today: old scents and new magic. I feel you, human. Your scent is on the wind. I am Grubark."

Aria pressed her finger warningly to her lips. "Oh go back to bed you rotting slug," she said loudly. "You're dumb as a cow and blind as a rock. There's no one here but me."

A deep rumble rose from Grubark's belly. "Do not try me, little fairy. I smell his flesh, I heard him speak."

"You're an old ugly mule; you're dreaming things. I played by a Gate today. Perhaps some human magic leaked through."

The grotesque blob twisted and expanded. "Do not interfere! The human boy is mine!"

Aria drew in a sharp breath. "Tavin, run!"

Tavin needed no further warning. He turned and sprinted away from the water. An eruption of stale breath and mucus blasted him to his knees. Tavin scrambled forward in a mad dash for firmer ground.

He reached a line of short, thick-trunked trees. He stopped to catch his breath, rubbing the stitch in his side. A cry of outrage turned his attention back to the water.

Hundreds of tentacles thrust out through Grubark's lumber-mill jaws. Aria ducked and slashed with her magical blades. A tentacle caught her by the ankle and whipped her high into the air. She fought fiercely upside-down, but could no longer reach the creature. Grubark thrashed her down into the water as if trying to snap her spine.

Tavin's heart burned. His hand closed around a sharp rock and he threw it with all his might. The rock bruised and cut Grubark's wrinkled skin, leaving behind weeping yellow sores. He found more, pitching them as quickly as he could.

Grubark twisted with rage. His tentacles shot towards Tavin and ripped the tree that sheltered him out of the earth. Tavin slid behind the cover of a log, rocks and clods of dirt raining down around his ears.

"Tavin!" Grubark whipped Aria out of the water and hung her by her ankles high in the air. Aria's yells came to a halt. Her face turned pale. From his hiding place, Tavin could see Grubark catch her arms and pin them to her sides.

Tavin opened his knife and ran for the water. His heart pounded like a jackhammer. Pink tentacles shot towards him and whipped above his head as Tavin dove into the swamp. Weighed down by the stones in his pockets, Tavin sunk as he swam towards the monster.

As he dropped away from the surface, the water grew clearer. Far below, the rocky swamp bed glowed with soft green luminescence.

Grubark's decomposing bulk writhed before him. Long tentacles snaked out of a fleshy orifice, securing Grubark to the roots of swamp trees.

Tavin clawed his way deeper and attacked the round lump near the base of the monster. Yellow fluid seeped from the wounds, poisoning the water.

Grubark shuddered, his tentacles lancing towards Tavin like arrows. Tavin curled into a ball and sunk further. He rolled onto his side and swam hard to his left. Once again, he struck with his knife, tearing through the hide.

His lungs bursting, Tavin dropped the rocks and thrashed upwards. He broke the surface and sucked in air. Water slapped into his mouth as the swamp shook with a sudden violent explosion. Then something snagged his ankle, pulling him under.

A second creature, dark red and squid-like, tore through the hole Tavin had slashed and out of Grubark's belly. Grubark shrieked and fell into the swamp. The squid creature latched hungrily onto Tavin's leg, pulling him in a deadly embrace.

The water tasted sweet and rotten. The skin of the squid creature glowed — pale and cold like a corpse — brightening as its tentacles crushed the air from Tavin's lungs.

Tavin fought back fiercely. He freed his right arm and buried his knife into a large fish-like eye.

The squid creature writhed in pain. It gave a long pitiful wail and released him, fleeing into the secret depths of the swamp.

Tavin's jeans and coat dragged him towards the bottom. His lungs screamed for air but each time he tried to swim towards the surface, sharp pain shot through his side, crippling his stroke.

He clenched his teeth, his determination to live smashing

through the pain. He thrashed upwards, reaching for the surface. A white hand broke through the water and closed over his wrist. Tavin kicked a few more times and surfaced with a choking gasp.

Tavin collapsed upon the sandy shore, trembling and spewing tainted water from his injured lungs. Aria held him, stroking his hair back from his face, a crooked grin pulling on the corners of her mouth.

"Not bad for a human," she said.

Glossymer Fields

"What were those things?" he asked.

"Grubark is another Chill," Aria said. "Like Madame Caveat, he lives by paralyzing his prey with poison and draining the blood. But instead of murdering outright like Caveat, Grubark earns his living by guarding the way to our village. In exchange, we give him gifts to keep him fat and slow."

"That was slow?"

Aria flashed her fangs. "I think you caused it to go into premature labor."

"Oh, gross," Tavin groaned. He rolled to his feet, gripping a tree root to ride out a dizzy spell. There didn't seem to be enough oxygen in the air. Thinking the pain in his side was nothing but a bad stitch, he pressed his arm against his ribs.

"Which way?" he asked.

"Tavin, stand still. You're bleeding." Aria gripped his arm to steady him.

Tavin looked down at the red smudge spreading through his dirty tee shirt. "Oh."

Aria sucked air between her teeth. "It's the poison. It numbs any wounds you have. You never realize you're hurt until it's too late."

"I'm fine."

Aria tapped her foot. "Take off your shirt."

"No."

"Oh, shut up and let me see."

Tavin let her tug off his shirt. His head hurt and he felt thirsty, which was strange considering how much swamp water he'd swallowed.

An ugly black barb protruded from his side, its jagged edges held fast in Tavin's torn flesh. Aria drew in another sharp breath.

"I'm not a healer," she said. "If I pull it out, I'll make a mess of it. The barbs will tear your skin and the wound will become worse. If I leave it in, it'll fester."

Aria couldn't resist. Her fingers found his scar.

Tavin pulled away before she could shock him.

His fingers twitched, missing their rubber band.

"My village is close," Aria said. "If we can get to the book, I can heal you."

Tavin tore his ragged shirt and used it to tie a crude bandage. Aria helped him back into his army jacket and found a stout branch for him to lean on. Tavin took a slow breath and forced himself to smile.

"Let's go."

They walked through swirling eddies of fog and past trees with long grasping branches. Pools of murky water and sinking sand honeycombed the ground beneath a carpet of weeds. Bulbous pods oozed from cracks in trees. Tavin brushed against one and it burst, coating the side of his head with mucus. Aria stopped to wipe his face with her sleeve.

Evening passed and the night deepened into the darkness of a tar pit. Even with little light, Aria moved confidently from one dry patch of land to another. Tavin's breath labored in his chest, expelling in shallow gasps. Finally he stopped, leaning on his staff. Aria traveled a ways before noticing he was no longer with her. She turned back.

"It's not far now," she said.

"Just give me a moment." Tavin leaned wearily against a tree, hardly even caring when a fleshy pod burst against his elbow.

Aria touched his face, her expression betraying a flicker of concern. "You don't look so good — for a human."

Tavin let his head fall back against the tree, savoring the chance to rest.

Aria pinched him hard on the arm, her eyes wide. "Don't do that," she hissed. "It's not safe. What if you don't wake up?"

Tavin shook his head trying to clear the cobwebs that tangled his brain.

"Fine." Aria gripped his arm. "You rest. I'm going to go ahead and get some things to help. Wait for me, and don't you dare pass out."

Tavin nodded. Aria slid away and vanished into the gray fog. The darkness closed behind her; the night became as still as a tomb.

Tavin shivered and pulled his jacket closed. He'd spent little time alone in the wild, but he had the distinct impression that he should be able to hear something. He'd seen a jungle on TV before. It had been alive with screeching birds and little animals rushing through the bushes. The swamp reminded him of the jungle, but he could hear nothing. The silence itself was a physical force. The crushing blackness leaned against him. Tavin found himself trying to breathe as quietly as possible.

All at once, he began to feel the night wasn't empty at all. It was alive, alert, and stalking him. A massive presence lurked just beyond the edges of darkness: something more dangerous than anything he'd encountered yet. Tavin's head began to pound. If headaches were a sign of his gift trying to tell him something, it'd just gone into overdrive.

Tavin leaned forward, straining to hear something from the darkness. Not a leaf stirred, but the presence grew so strong he felt he could touch it. He held his breath, and at last he heard it: a whisper from the night. It moved through the trees like a snake through grass; it sounded like words.

"Tavin!" A hand clamped heavily down on his mouth, stifling his cry. Aria hissed. "What's wrong?"

Tavin peeled her hand away. "There's something out there," he said. "I could feel it."

"There's nothing. This place has been dead for centuries." Aria passed him a bundle from under her arm. "Here," she said. "This was the best I could do."

He held a skin of water wrapped in a grey cloak. He opened the skin and drank greedily. Aria draped the cloth over his shoulders. Tavin scanned the trees again, but the menacing presence he'd felt was gone.

Aria's hands trembled as she laced the cloak up around Tavin's neck. "In and out," she said. "If you slouch, no one will notice your height. The book lies below the temple and the temple is never guarded. Most fairies don't even know the book exists."

"And there's a spell to heal my sister?"

"And you. I told you, it's a record of magic almost as old as our worlds. It'll be easy," she said. "It's been four hundred years."

"Since what?"

Aria gnawed her cheek. "The last time anyone's seen a human. They'll never expect it."

Tavin cracked a weary smile. "You're not afraid, are you?"

Aria's lips tightened. She handed him his staff. "Put on the hood," she said. "Make sure your face remains hidden and remember to hunch. Don't speak."

"Don't speak. Got it." Tavin gripped his staff tightly, feeling a rush of exhilaration that for a moment made him forget the danger. Impulsively, he kissed Aria on the cheek. She didn't pull away, so he kissed her gently on the lips. She pulled up her hood with a small smile. "Let's go."

The ground began to slope upwards and became noticeably dryer. Wafts of clean, sweet-smelling air drifted past them. The rubbery trunks of swamp trees gave way to tall slender trees with smooth pale bark. Clustered together high in the air, the branches glowed with gray ghostly light.

As they drew closer, Tavin saw something like thick cobwebs cocooning the trees and casting the light. Unlike Madame Caveat's tight and heavy spider webs, these strands tumbled from the branches and dropped to the ground, twisting and billowing back towards the sky at the slightest breeze. High above, slender bridges plunged and soared in gravity-defying arcs, linking the trees together. Silver wind chimes and chunks of bright crystal that spat rainbows dangled from the branches.

Their tired feet sank down into fragrant beds of moss. Bright explosions of rainbow colors flickered above their heads. Tavin heard voices, faint and indistinct. Aria's wings fluttered eagerly behind her, shimmering pale blue.

"Walking is so unnatural," she muttered. "You can't see anything from down here."

"What's in the trees?" Tavin asked.

"Glossymer beds," Aria said. "The spindle worm weaves the

silk among the leaves and we harvest it. Our village has the largest spindle colony in the swamp. That's why Mya is here."

"Mya?"

Aria pointed.

They'd drawn near a clearing and the trees parted to give them a clear view of the sky. Cresting the top of the hill and snagging the stars among its branches was the biggest tree Tavin had ever imagined. It grew hundreds of feet into the air and looked as thick around as Teilenheim Village. Its branches acted like roadways to spindly towers, woven like wooden baskets with the appearance of inverted beehives. Wide footpaths, wrapped in blue and white strings of glossymer, twisted in spidery pathways around Mya's dark, corded trunk. Small warm lights winked from gaps in the bark. Hundreds of dark figures on brightly colored wings danced in spirals about the tree as fairies flew to and from its great height.

"It's beautiful," Tavin's mouth hung in unabashed awe.

"She's a true friend," Aria said softly. "When the spindle worms die, they nourish her soul with their small magics. In return, Mya protects them from predators. She protects us as well. My entire clan lives in Mya's bark and branches. "

Tavin looked at the giant tree with deepening respect. The thought of it being alive sent a shiver down his spine. He never wanted to make something so massive angry with him.

"Why are there so many fairies awake? Don't they sleep?"

"Nightshift," replied Aria. "Glossymer is used for more than spinning wings, and the spindle worms take a lot of looking after.

But don't worry — it's quieter in the temple."

She nodded in a different direction. At the far end of the clearing, beneath the shadow of bare pine trees, sprawled a large crumbling cathedral lit from within by dull silver light. Wooden beams jutted out above the walls, marking the place where the roof had been. Tall stained glass windows cast eerie shadows upon the lawn. A bell tower teetered far off center, causing Tavin to wonder if magic held it fast. The cathedral seemed forgotten and sacred at the same time, glittering like a discarded diamond.

Tavin started forward and stumbled, much to his surprise. He'd forgotten about the poisoned barb.

Aria glanced towards his side.

"Don't worry," he said. "I can't feel anything."

"It's bad when you do," she replied. "Let's go around the clearing and keep to the shadows. Someone might wonder why we're walking."

They hurried through the trees, moving from the shelter of one trunk to another and away from the glossymer fields. About halfway to the cathedral, something tore in Tavin's side. Blood ran down his pant leg. He tripped, catching himself on his staff and took a moment to gather his resolve. He'd cheated death before; he'd do it again.

The last stretch to the entrance of the church offered no further cover. Aria glanced nervously into the sky and ventured tentatively across the mossy clearing. Tavin followed the best he could, scanning the trees for movement.

The church steps were wide and cumbersome, worn smooth in the middle from centuries of feet passing over the rock.

Tavin nearly fell as he climbed. Aria grabbed his arm and helped him back to his feet. "We have to stop," she said.

He hunched over, pressing his hand against his side. "Don't worry about me, I'll make it."

"No!" Aria hissed. "You're leaving a trail," she said. "Only humans bleed red. If someone sees it we'll be caught!"

Tavin let himself rest on one knee, still holding his staff. He looked over his shoulder. She was right: a thin dark trail marked the place where they'd dashed from the woods and dotted the steps he'd just climbed.

"Well, what do you suggest? At least it's dark enough to hide the color."

"Something doesn't feel right." Aria gnawed on a nail.

Tavin stared at her in bafflement. He'd never seen her so skittish.

"We hide," she whispered at last. "We find a place to stitch you up and we wait for a better night."

"I could be dead by then! Poison, remember?"

"Who lingers on the steps?"

The voice spoke from overhead. Aria jumped. Tavin ducked his head low, tightening his grip upon his staff.

"I thought the king's orders were clear. Nightshift must gather for Council." The voice neared. Tavin heard the light sound of feet alighting upon the stone. How many had come? Two? Three?

"Please," Aria's voice quaked. She sounded pitiful. "Please, I must help my sick grandfather. He is too old to attend."

A short pause, followed by a low chuckle, answered her plea.

Tavin took a quick look.

There were four of them. They hovered in the air, dressed in pale golden armor trimmed with dark red. Each fairy carried a sword strapped to his waist. Bright eyes glimmered through the narrow slits in their masks.

The leader moved towards Aria. Tavin tensed and her grip on his arm tightened in warning.

"What's this," said the guard, "an old wingless peasant and his pretty granddaughter, soiling the sacred steps?" He reached out and yanked back Aria's hood. All four guards burst into laughter.

"By the stone, princess! You stink! Where have you been? Hiding in a swamp?"

Tavin almost fell over with shock. Princess?

Aria barred her teeth. "Stay away from me."

The guard snickered.

"On second thought" he said, "I don't want to know. You're in enough trouble already. You missed your brother's ceremony. Your father is furious."

Aria bristled. Her eyes flashed. If she was afraid, she no longer showed it.

"I'm not going back. I care about my father's wishes as much as he does mine. The ceremony is meaningless anyway. I've got twice the magic Axim does!"

The guard slapped her, his gauntleted hand leaving a red welt across her cheek and knocking her down. When Tavin moved to help her, she shook her head fiercely.

"Practicing magic again?" said the guard.

"Your father has been too kind. No female will ever be a mage; you should be beaten for thinking it."

Aria's voice shook with temper. She rose slowly to her feet. "Try it," she said, "and I'll kill you."

The guard laughed and grabbed Aria by the arm, dragging her down the steps. Despite her threats, Aria didn't fight back. Instead, she locked eyes with Tavin in warning. With a hum like giant bees, a second guard grabbed her other arm and pulled her into the air.

Seconds later Tavin felt strong hands grip his shoulders. He shifted his weight to his feet, ready to swing his staff, groaning like an old sick man.

"Come on, peasant," said the guard, "into the temple with the rest of them. And you'd better stay clear of the princess from now on, she almost got you arrested." He barked with laughter. "Some royal favor!"

They hoisted Tavin to his feet with a jerk and flew him up the stairs. Tavin heard a scraping moan as the heavy wooden doors swung inwards. He could see little in the dimness beyond.

The guards tossed him into the church like a sack of flour. Tavin collapsed upon the floor with the taste of blood in his mouth. He felt a shot of blossoming pain and realized the numbing had begun to wear off. It felt as if someone were sawing through his side with a dull knife.

What would they think, if they found him dead in their temple? What would happen to Aria?

He heard the guard's voices mocking him beyond the doors.

"You're fat," one cried, "and ugly! You nearly tore my wings!"

"Keep your dirty hands away from our princess!" another said. "If you know what's good for you! We won't have a fat peasant soiling the bloodline!"

As the great doors swung shut, Tavin heard one last comment.

"What's this on the steps? Berry juice? Ugh! It smells rotten. Must be something the princess dragged from the swamp. Make sure it's gone before the king arrives."

Then the doors closed, leaving Tavin alone.

The Human Threat

"The trouble with humans is that they do not know when to quit."

A stern voice boomed loudly from deeper within the church. A pale flickering light glowed beyond the wide foyer. On his hands and knees, Tavin dragged himself away from the doors and into a corner where shadows covered him like a cloak, embracing him with a cool earthy scent.

"They are impulsive, ill-tempered, violent, and deceitful," the speaker said.

Tavin shuddered. He couldn't stop his limbs from shaking. He wiped his mouth with the back of his hand, tasting blood.

"Come on, old-timer, up on your feet." The new voice sounded friendly, but Tavin knew otherwise. He had no friends here.

A bright light flashed across his face. Tavin cowered, letting his hood fall forward. Hands reached down and grabbed his arms, pulling him up.

"What 'ave ye found?" a female asked, sharp and full of curiosity.

"… came in late, and the temple guards gave 'im a rough time for it."

"They are an immoral species," the speaker shouted. "If we are not vigilant they can appear out of nowhere, bringing their lies and depravity with them."

A muffled shout of agreement rang through the inner sanctuary. Tavin was lead forward into a large room tightly packed with hot angry bodies.

"Who have you got there, Tamas?"

"Don't know 'im. Just some old-timer. Got the wind knocked out of 'im."

"Poor thing," warbled an elderly female. "'ere love, sit a spell."

Kind hands helped Tavin down onto a broad stone. He cringed, trying to slow the bleeding by wrapping his arms around his middle.

Cool earth lay beneath his feet. The pale light came from a round silver ball floating above their heads. Fairies borne on translucent wings and wearing silky robes flittered high among the rafters. A rougher-dressed crowd jostled one another upon the ground.

At the back of the church, a hook-nosed fairy with red butterfly wings paced upon a raised dais of stone.

"History," the fairy bellowed, "is our witness. When our world fractured in two, the Starbreather wisely stripped the human side of magic." The fairy leaned forward, his eyes gleaming. "These so-called 'human mages' are nothing but an unnatural mistake. They contain all the treacherous qualities of regular humans, but wield power never intended to be theirs. Once, we trusted them. Never again."

Tavin felt like a leper. On every side, fairies nodded in agreement, clapping and calling out in approval.

"Fear them," the fairy said. "Fear their sly tongues and eager promises. The word of a human is like hot wind. It scours the fields and scorches the harvest, leaving only emptiness." He paused. "None of you has seen a human before, but I assure you, they are monstrous."

The deep clanging of church bells interrupted the fairy's ugly sermon. The crowd grew still, looking up with expectation. The fairies in the rafters began to titter and jostle one another for a better look.

Tavin risked a look, squinting his eyes against the light of the silver globe. Gradually he made out the silhouette of a wide platform, carried by eight golden-armored guards, floating down from the sky. It carried two fairies, both with golden circlets upon their brows.

The first was tall, his wrinkled hands grasping a gnarled staff.

His sharp features and crooked nose gave him a hard shrewd appearance. His green-eyed gaze looked as if it could cut glass.

The second fairy was shorter, younger, and almost plump. His cheeks and lips were rosy pink and his hair pale blond. He wore shimmering lilac wings. He smiled pleasantly, but as he looked down upon the crowd, Tavin felt his heart skip a beat. The fairy's eyes gleamed red.

The golden guards settled the platform upon the raised dais. The older fairy stamped his staff and the assembly fell silent.

"I have gathered you, gentle-fairies, to speak on a grave matter," he said. "Our suspicions are confirmed. Humans have returned to Etheria."

The crowd gasped. A fairy beside Tavin jumped to his feet in such agitation that he knocked Tavin to the ground. For a dangerous few seconds Tavin's hood fell back, exposing features too rough for a fairy. Tavin yanked the hood over his head and cowed in pain, unable to rise.

"It's true." The younger fairy nodded to the older one and flew into the air. "Human magic has shaken our Gates. Two nights ago Goblintown was attacked."

A few snorts sounded from the crowd. The young fairy raised his arm with a sympathetic smile, his red eyes sweeping the crowd. "There is more," he said. "The swamp guardian that guards these borders is dead, and the swamp is filled with the bloody marks of a man. No mere human could have fought Grubark and survived; we are convinced this is the work of a mage."

An angry rolling mutter passed through the assembly.

The older fairy thumped his staff. "Order!" His voice dropped with heaviness. "In times like these, even our enemies may become friends. The prince has found a witness."

The gathered crowd grew silent. Tavin became aware of a low clicking noise echoing up from somewhere beneath the cathedral floor. He pulled himself through the crowd and onto a pile of stone rubble. Over the heads of the crowd, he could now see a low arched doorway sunken into the ground beneath the dais at the front.

The noise grew louder, accompanied by a rustle and a long scraping sound. A moment later, a tattered shadow crawled out from the darkness of the doorway. Tavin saw an old woman, dressed in rags, her body swinging sideways as her long spider legs dragged her up onto the stage. The speaker on the stage drew back in revulsion. The old king's expression darkened and the crowd shifted uneasily. Only the prince remained unfazed.

"Madame, speak your tale," the prince said.

"Murderer!" a voice cried. "Monster!"

"Peace, my people!" the king ordered. "She has purchased safe passage," he turned to Madame Caveat with a canny gaze. "... for tonight."

Madame Caveat grinned, showing off a mouthful of rotten teeth. "The humans crossed the divide and fought with magic," she pronounced. "I've seen it with my own poor eyes." She unfurled a stumpy black leg. "They did this to me!"

The crowd shifted uneasily.

Madame Caveat was a known fairy killer. If it were anyone but a human mage, he would have received the highest honors for such a deed.

"This proves beyond doubt that human magic is alive and well," the king said. "The ancient treaty has been broken." He looked across the crowd. "My people, we have come to the threshold of war."

Tavin slipped and fell heavily to the ground. Blood pounded in his ears. He tried to rise, but the press of the crowd kept him down. He bled freely now, staining the ground he crawled on.

The king griped the jeweled sword hilt at his waist. "It is time to make a stand. The human world outnumbers us ten to one. We must act to curb this threat now before it grows too late."

Tavin made it back to his feet. The king continued to speak over the crowd, but Tavin felt a change in the air. He raised his head slowly, the hair on his arms prickling as if touched by a low electric shock.

The prince watched him, a slight frown upon his face. Tavin pressed against the crowd, hoping to disappear. The prince saw him move. His keen gaze locked onto Tavin like laser points.

A scream cut the air behind Tavin. A fairy near to the pile of stones held up a red palm.

"Blood!" she cried. "It's human blood!"

The crowd parted like water. Tavin stumbled for cover but tripped and fell against someone, leaving a long crimson smudge against the fairy's tunic. The blond prince moved quickly, his finger thrust forward. The crowd separated further, stampeding towards the door.

A bright bolt of purple lightning shot out of the prince's finger towards Tavin. Tavin swung his staff up. The purple beam slammed into the wooden staff and shattered it into a thousand pieces. The explosion flung Tavin backwards against the wall. He hit the ground and tried to rise but couldn't get his arms or legs to work. He remained where he'd fallen: facedown, a wide stain spreading beneath him.

Golden guards grabbed his arms and hauled him upright. They pulled his hood off.

Those who remained in the cathedral gasped in horror. The world pin-wheeled around Tavin in bright colors and silver shadows. He locked on the old king and the flash of the prince's red eyes. The prince took hold of his head and forced it up. Standing safely back, Madame Caveat screeched with laughter.

"Not a mage, but definitely human," the prince said. "He had help to come this far. Father?"

The old king nodded. "Do what you must, Axim."

The prince let go of Tavin's jaw. "Lock him away."

Tavin's vision tunneled until he could make nothing out but the prince's eyes. Then, like a light switching out, his mind fell into darkness.

Captured

*H*e woke because he was thirsty, and because of the pain in his arms. Dim morning light fell in chunks from above, painting the dirt floor beneath him in stripes.

Tavin shook his hair from his eyes and struggled into a sitting position. Rope bound his arms behind his back. Strapped into his left arm was something very much like an IV, fed from a large gourd dangling from the ceiling. Tavin took a ragged breath and winced with pain from the wound in his side. His tattered army jacket hung open from his shoulders, clearly displaying the deep scar in his chest. He looked down and saw that the wound in his side had been stitched shut with thick black thread.

Tavin looked up. What he'd first thought were bars were actually roots. They formed a roof about twenty feet up and threaded their way downwards, reinforcing the earthen walls of his cell in a wooden tangle.

A shadow passed overhead and someone shoved a piece of rotten fruit through the roots, hitting him in the face. A bark of laughter was followed by more rotten fruit and several eel heads. Tavin ducked and gritted his teeth, tugging on the ropes around his wrists.

A narrow wooden door, bound with iron, opened behind him. Tavin turned to glower angrily at the woman that stepped through. She held a washing basin and clean bandages in her hands. Her clothing was coarse grey in color and her feet were bare. A stocky guard with a steel breastplate and a short brown tunic followed her in.

The woman baulked at seeing Tavin awake. The guard fingered the baton he carried as the woman timidly cleaned and bandaged Tavin's side. Tavin remained as still as a stone, his eyes locked upon the guard's.

"Why am I here?" he said. "Why did you tie me up?"

The deep lines around the guard's mouth tightened slightly, but otherwise he made no response.

Tavin looked up at the woman tending him. "Did I hurt you or your family?" he demanded. "Do you know what I've done?" The woman flinched as she fastened the last of the bandages. She fumbled for the things she'd brought with her and fled from the cell.

Tavin's heart beat fast and hot in his chest. When the guard slammed the door shut, Tavin ground his teeth so hard his jaw ached. He heard a heavy bolt slide into place.

"You can't just leave me here!" he yelled. "I've done nothing wrong!" Tavin kicked the door and slumped against the ground. He laughed in low shallow pain. He supposed he should be afraid, but his mind buzzed angrily, pushing back the fear and replacing it with bitterness. He dropped his head to his knees, his heart yearning for home.

Moreanna had found him in the fire the night his mom died. He would have died too if she hadn't known where to look. Instead, Moreanna led the fire fighters right to him.

Later, in the hospital, she'd cried for him. Tavin's tears had been burned up in the fire with the last of his mom's screams, but she'd held his hand and cried, soothing the rage that ate away at him from inside. Tavin's sides shook. Moreanna was the brave one, not him. She'd faced the pain of losing mom for both of them. Physical pain he could handle, but it was the anger he ran from.

Tavin forced himself to take a slow deep breath. It'd been harder when dad left. Moreanna had seemed distant somehow, but in the end, she'd been there for him. She'd shown him that they could still be strong together, that the bond they shared was enough.

Now Moreanna was little more that a wishful echo in his mind. She was blocked somehow, now when he needed her the most. It wasn't the guards that scared him—it was the darkness that slid about in his brain, a darkness that Moreanna had stood against for so many years and pushed back with the light and strength of her love. Now Tavin was alone, and the darkness was stronger.

The guard returned just as the daylight began to fade towards evening. Four more guards, these ones dressed in breastplates and helmets of royal gold, followed close behind. A hot ball of fire rolled around in Tavin's belly. They'd abandoned him for a whole day: bound and in pain, without food or water.

The guards released him long enough to relieve himself in the corner of the cell. Tavin could hardly feel his hands. Once he'd finished, they retied his wrists tightly behind his back.

"Can I get some water?" he asked.

They ignored him, shoving him out of the cell and down a long hallway. The floor smelt like mildew, and the walls were built of entwining roots. Clear round bowls, set high in the walls, flickered with weak greenish flame.

Tavin shoved with his shoulder at the back of the nearest guard.

"Hey, I need a drink!"

The guard turned and struck Tavin, throwing him against the wall. Tavin twisted about and jumped at the guard, knocking the fairy to the ground. Tavin fell with his heel against the fairy's throat. A metal fist cuffed him from behind. Tavin, stunned and in pain, was dragged back to his feet. Low laughter echoed through the hall. Tavin raised his pounding head as a section of the roots unraveled and pulled apart forming a doorway. Tavin raised his chin to meet the eyes of the red-eyed prince. He wore a bright red cape draped across his chest and over one shoulder.

"So, the human has some fight left!" The prince's voice was both as smooth as honey and sharp as iron. "Stop that abuse and bring him along. Send someone to get him some water at once."

Through the doorway, a sharp flight of spiraling stairs climbed up into uncertain darkness. The prince led the way, his hand glowing with a deep purple light. Tavin, weak and still dizzy with pain, climbed for what felt like hours. He fell several times, banging his shins and sliding backwards. Finally, two cursing guards hauled him up by his arms and carried him the rest of the way. They came at last to a door made of green wood, which the prince opened using a large black key. Hot sunlight hit Tavin in the face as he was carried through. The guards dropped him down on a wooden chair and left.

It took some time for Tavin's eyes to adjust to the light. Gradually he was able to make out that he sat in the center of a wide, round room. Half the room was built of carved wooden columns rather than walls, and it opened directly towards the red setting sun. Everything in the room, from floor to ceiling, was made of honey-colored tree bark and gleamed with a smooth polished finish.

Four tall thrones sat with their backs to the sun and cast long dark shadows into the room. The prince settled himself comfortably on the far right and considered Tavin with canny interest.

A servant girl brought Tavin a bowl of water and helped him to drink. She also washed his face and combed his hair.

The prince studied him for some time, his head cocked to one side. His smile was as cold as winter rain. "Well, human, this is your lucky day. Despite my better judgment, I've decided not to make an example of you. Instead, I'm going to give you a wish."

Tavin head felt like thick porridge. He wondered if he'd heard right. "A what?"

"Like in human fairytales," the prince said. "The human catches a fairy and gets a wish, only this time," the prince smirked, "I've caught you. Tell me human, what do you wish for most in the world?"

The last thing Tavin wanted was to tell his greatest wish to the slimeball in front of him. All he could think of was Opa's warning not to trust fairies, and he was almost certain this one had it out for him. Still — if there was a chance, he had to take it.

"My sister," he said, "she's sick." His tongue felt like a stone. "I wish for her to be well."

The prince raised his eyebrows and examined his fingernails. "No riches, power, or secrets? You know that magic is good for much more than curing a cough."

"Nothing else."

The prince sighed extravagantly. "I've never actually seen a human before," he said. "Even beneath those bruises I can tell you're not as different from us as everyone hoped. If anything, you seem fragile, like a giant made of clay. Your wish is an easy one to grant, but — of course there will be a cost."

"I came alone."

The prince laughed. He blew upon his fingertips causing them to glow with violet light. "I can see you don't fully understand your situation." He paused. "Did you know that human mages are among the most powerful of us? Ironic, isn't it? I'm not even sure I could challenge an actual human mage on my own. No, to win a fight like that I would need something special. I'm talking about your scar, of course." The prince's eyes flickered covetously towards Tavin's chest. "You're no master; I doubt you know how to use whatever magic lays dormant inside of you. You're simply an apprentice. The mage that shakes the earth — now him I've heard about."

"I came alone," replied Tavin stubbornly. "There's no one else. I know nothing about an Earth mage."

The prince waved his hand. "There will be time for that later," he said. He leaned forward. "Serve me. Stay here and train. I can help you unlock the secrets inside of you, and you can help me defend this kingdom. And of course, I will heal your sister from every sickness that has ever touched her. It will be as if she has a new body."

"I didn't know this kingdom was yours to defend."

The prince's smile was sickly sweet. "Not yet." His fingers glowed brighter. He pointed and a bolt of fire struck Tavin in the chest. The blast knocked Tavin backwards and off his chair, but once Tavin recovered his breath, he noticed with surprise that the bolt had done little more than stun him. The scar on his chest tingled with warmth.

The prince rose to his feet and peered at Tavin with a quizzical look. "Interesting," he said. His fingers began to glow once again.

"Regardless, I will have your secrets, if not your loyalty."

Tavin forced himself to meet the prince's eyes, steeling himself for what was to come.

A low thrumming sound interrupted them. The prince turned his head and the light in his fingers flashed out. Moments later, three bright silhouettes landed smoothly among the columns in the room.

The first to land was the craggy-faced king. Upon his arm, a slender woman with fiery red hair and a hunched back leaned for support. Aria landed several steps behind them and two steps ahead of a golden-armored escort.

Her skin glowed like snow against the pale blue of her dress. A glittering thread of gemstones swept her dark red hair off her neck. Tavin sucked in a startled breath and hurriedly looked away.

"What have you done, Axim?" Aria snapped. Her eyes met Tavin's for the brief flash of a second. She hurriedly looked away. "You were supposed to meet us at Mya's core."

The prince relaxed, flopping back down into his chair. "Father asked me to speak with the human, see if I could earn its trust and find out who its accomplice was."

"And did you?"

"Sadly, no." Axim's gaze grew dull, his lids dropped to hood his glowing eyes. He sniffed and lazed back as if what happened next held no interest for him.

The king turned his head sharply. "You are too soft, my son. You must learn that a king should also be feared." The king pointed towards Tavin. "Secure the human," he commanded.

Three guards tied Tavin to the chair. Tavin didn't fight back. He was having a hard time keeping his eyes off Aria.

The queen sniffed. "How vulgar, it smells like rotten cabbage."

"Ready yourself, my dear, this is for the kingdom." The king narrowed his eyes at Tavin, a look Tavin recognized from Aria. "Make no mistake, human," the king said. "This is your last interview. If I am satisfied with your answers, I will cut out your eyes and allow you to live as my pet. If not, I will cleanse this world of one more human."

"Father!" Aria's cheeks flushed with anger.

A slow smile moved across Axim's face. He raised a questioning eyebrow at his sister.

"Silence!" The king held up his hands. "You will learn how a king rules." The king pointed his staff towards Tavin. "Speak, human. Why have you invaded my court?"

Tavin's throat felt like sand paper. He pushed back the bile rising in his throat. "I've done nothing wrong."

"You've ignored a four hundred year old treaty. You've attacked my subjects and trespassed on sacred ground." The king leaned forward. "And you had help. Who is your accomplice?"

"No one."

"No mere human fights off swamp creatures alone," the king said. "You reek of magic, spy, but it is not yours. I will ask you one last time: who is helping you?"

The question hung in the air an electric moment. Tavin forced himself to look at the king and no one else. "I came alone," he said.

Axim sniffed. "Cover your eyes, mother."

One of the guards pulled Tavin up by his hair and struck him in the face with a gauntleted fist. Tavin, biting back a gasp, felt his nose crack and slide. White pain blanked out his vision. Tavin sucked air, dropping his head. A second blow to his side tore stitches and burst open the wound. They struck him again across the face, forcing unwanted tears to blur Tavin's vision. Blood ran from a gash over his eye. Both his eyes began to swell closed. Tavin clenched his jaw. He felt the darkness that haunted him move quietly into place.

Desperate, Tavin dared a glimpse through swollen eyes at the Aria. The setting sun enshrouded her with light. She looked like an angel. He closed his eyes and fixed the image in his mind, using it to battle back the darkness.

"Father," Aria trembled as she rose from her chair, but set her feet stubbornly. "I have heard a prophecy. The Unmaker seeks to return."

The pain stopped. The guards backed away, unsure of what to do. Tavin gasped for breath. He called to mind the memory of flying with Aria, her hair red like phoenix feathers.

"Now is not the time or place, Aria," the king replied.

"You would not let me come to you earlier; I had no choice but to wait until now. Surely the Unmaker is a greater threat than a single broken human."

"Nonsense," the king said. "It's impossible." But his words seemed uncertain.

"And what was the Unmaker but a stinking human?" Axim drawled.

Aria's face paled. "It was the humans who saved us from him," she said. "What if they've only come back to help?"

"I doubt it," replied the queen. "You can never trust a human."

"And you would defend them?" Axim raised his eyebrows at Aria. "I also know my history, sister. How many Etharians died in a war they started?"

"They saved us," Aria repeated.

Axim smirked. "Careful, sister," he said. "Someone might think you've been spending time with them."

Aria dug her fingers in to the arms of her chair, small blue sparks began to arc across her fingers. Axim's eyes brightened beneath his dropped lids.

"That's enough!" the king roared. A large white stone upon a chain around his neck shimmered with a flash of pearly colors. Instantly Axim's eyes darkened to the color of dried blood and Aria's blue sparks vanished, leaving behind the slight smell of sulfur.

The king pinched his long nose as if in pain. "Perhaps you are right, daughter; rumors of the Unmaker must take first priority. A live demon is a greater threat to this kingdom than a dead human."

Aria's face drained from angry red to white.

"Return the human to his cell," the king commanded. "Make sure it's secure. If it hasn't told us anything by morning, cut its throat and be done with it."

Prince Axim turned his face up and sniffed. "Smells like rain," he said. He laughed. "Sleep well, human."

Mya's Chamber

The first drops of rain came with the night. They fell in a few heavy splatters against Tavin's skin then turned into a shower.

Hours passed. The bottom of his cell turned to mud. With his arms still tied, Tavin could find no comfortable way to lie. His head pounded with pain from his broken nose. It felt like a spike driven into his forehead. He turned his face towards the rain, letting the water wash the sticky blood away, catching a drink through his swollen lips.

He waited, knowing she'd come; knowing that she

shouldn't — that it could cost her both their lives — but knowing she'd come nonetheless.

She came.

A soft blue light roused Tavin from an exhausted slumber. He looked up. The tree roots that wove across the wall of his cell glowed brightly then slid sideways, pulling into the earth and forming a small dark doorway. Her eyes glowing green, Aria stepped through the hole. The roots slid back into place behind her and the door vanished.

Aria's hair hung in a stern braid down her back. She wore a close-fitting shirt and tight leggings, both in black. She offered him a brave smile as she freed his hands with a magic sword. Her blade cut through the bindings on his arms and wrists with the scent of ash.

"Princess," he said.

"I'm here," she whispered. "Shhh … it's okay now." Her eyes filled with tears. "I'm so sorry. I didn't know what to do." Aria dropped to her knees and pressed a cool cloth to his face. It smelt of mint and lilac. Tavin breathed deep, almost crying as he felt the pain of his broken nose ease. "My father thinks he's protecting us," she said. "He doesn't understand."

"I knew you'd come," Tavin whispered. His hands were shaking. "There's something inside me, Aria, something ugly. I felt it trying to get out — I almost let it." Tavin wrapped his arms around his side. The torn wound felt hot and swollen.

"Here." She passed him a flask from the bag she carried. "Drink this."

Tavin leaned against the cell wall for support. The liquid had a strong bitter taste. It sent a rush of warmth and strength through his limbs. Aria leaned forward and brushed her lips across his, her face hot. Despite the soreness of his cheeks, it sent a thrill through Tavin.

"If it wasn't for you," he said. "I think …" He shook his head. "I don't know what it was but it wanted to kill them." He buried his face into her neck, breathing in the scent of her hair. "But you're different."

Aria ran a hand down the side of his face. "Hush. You don't have to worry about them." She stroked his hair. "I'm going to get you out of here." She stood and walked back to the wall, pressing her palm flat against a thick tree root. Her eyes shut briefly and her lips moved as if she were talking, but no sound came out. Tavin felt a small tremor roll through the cell. With a protesting creak, the roots parted once again to make a door.

"How did you do that?" Tavin asked.

Aria smiled secretively. "It wasn't me," she replied. "It was Mya. She doesn't understand humans, but I've convinced her to make an exception. And I don't think she likes Axim much."

Aria slid her hand into Tavin's, and led him into the darkness beyond the doorway. Once they left the cell, the roots wound shut behind them, encasing them in a small damp room of earth and tree bark. Eerie green light seeped from the roots and lit the space around them. If there'd been a window or a torch, Tavin would have never noticed the light, but in the near darkness, it was just enough to trace the outlines of Aria's pale round face.

With a hand lovingly trailing across Mya's roots, Aria walked forward, bringing Tavin with her. The room reformed as they moved, opening the path before them and closing after they passed. The packed earth beneath their feet remained thoughtfully smooth and level.

They traveled in silence. The dim light and warmth of the chamber never changed, and it lulled Tavin into a dreamlike state. It was hard to guess the passage of time. When Aria finally stopped walking, she had to call Tavin's name several times to get his attention.

Mya parted her roots at eyelevel to form a narrow peephole into the world beyond. Tavin's nose twitched as the scent of cool air and damp grass flowed into the chamber, accompanied by gray moonlight. Aria pressed her cheek to the peephole. It seemed like an eternity had passed before she drew back.

"This is as far as Mya can take us," she whispered. "The outer wall of the prison is bored through stone. Luckily, we don't have to go towards the main gate. There's an air vent less than a hundred paces from here. The lock's old and should be easy to break. If all goes well, it'll be hours before anyone realizes we're gone."

Tavin nodded, itching to get out of the suffocating chamber and into cool air. The twisting roots were starting to make his skin crawl. Mya's mothering presence had begun to feel hot and oppressive. He licked his lips. "What are we waiting for?"

Aria took one last look into the room beyond. "Looks clear," she said. She concentrated for a moment, communicating with Mya. With a soft creak and a whoosh of air, the thick roots parted twisting into an arched doorway.

"I'll go first," Tavin stepped forward, surprising Aria. He left the chamber with a soft sigh of relief, feeling his head grow clearer with every deep lungful of air. He stood in an intersection of two hallways. Behind him, tree and earth burrowed into the ground; the passageway lit by flickering torches. Before him, forming a sharp 'T,' a stone passage cut across the earth in an abrupt, regular formation. Narrow slots in the ceiling of the stone passage threw bars of moonlight down onto the stone floor.

Tavin felt his way hungrily forward and pressed himself into the cool shadows of the arching stone passage. He turned his head to call for Aria, when he saw the guard. Her name died on his lips.

The prison guard's uniform of steel and dark leather had allowed him to blend into the stone walls. Whether by accident or intention Tavin had missed him. The guard, seeing movement, jerked to attention and swung a black-shafted spear towards Tavin's throat. A long string of strange words spilled angrily from his lips. Tavin dropped, kicking the guard's legs from under him. Without looking back, he jumped to his feet and raced around the corner towards the safety of Mya's hidden chamber.

The room was gone, and with it, Aria.

Tavin spun in desperation, determined not to run blindly deeper into the dungeon. Panic crawled up his throat. He'd rather die than go back to his cell. He pressed his back against the wall, his fingers running frantically across the coarse roots. The guard, as if to see him better, raised his mask up onto his forehead, revealing a face not much older than Tavin's and eyes, as clear as sapphires, sparking in anger.

A door formed and Aria stepped out from the wall behind the guard, her expression hard and bitter. The guard hesitated, sensing something was wrong.

Before he could react, Aria flicked her wrist, sending blue bolts of light arcing into his back. The force of her strike blew the guard back several feet. He slammed into the wall and dropped to the ground in soundless pain. He convulsed. His eyes rolled up into his head and foam dotted his lips. After a long horrible moment, he finally grew still.

"Is he dead?" The words cut Tavin's throat like razor blades.

Aria shrugged; her lips tight. She kicked the guard in the side and pointed to a red eye in a circle of gold, inscribed upon the guard's armored shoulder.

"He belongs to Axim's personal retinue." She sneered. "He deserved it." Aria turned and stalked towards the pale light of the stone hall. She didn't even look back to see if Tavin followed or not.

Pale greenish roots crept across the floor and wrapped about the guard's arms and ankles. Mya dragged the body into the prison wall and closed around behind him. Damp darkness devoured first his legs then his chest and then his entire body. Tavin retched and wiped his mouth. He turned and hurried after Aria, telling himself that the guard was not dead, only stunned, and Mya would take good care of him. He almost believed it.

The air vent proved to be a small round hole cut eight feet deep through the outer rock wall. To fit, Tavin had to twist his shoulders so that one arm reached out in front of his body and the other dragged by his hip. It was a narrow fit but he made it. Aria broke the lock upon the bars with a burst of blue fire and they both tumbled free onto a damp grassy slope.

The short grass embraced his weary limbs. Tavin shivered. His army coat, tattered and coated with mud, hung heavily across his shoulders with little warmth.

"Come," Aria said. "You can rest when it's safe."

Tavin followed Aria with a weary run deep into the woods beyond the prison. They passed into the thick of the forest and halted within a tight clump of young pines. As Tavin sank to the ground, Aria pulled a cloak from the small pack she carried, this one black, and wrapped it around his shoulders.

"I'm sorry you had to see that," she said at last. Her voice broke with sudden emotion. "I couldn't let them take you ... not again."

She almost sounded genuine. Tavin nodded numbly, relieved. He hung his head in exhaustion. The branches overhead were thick enough to shield them from the rain. Aria helped him drink some more from the flask she carried before reluctantly breaking the silence.

"Why didn't you tell my family about me?" she asked. "You could have saved your sister."

Tavin lowered the flask. The liquid in it sent fire burning through his limbs and pushed his mind into a state of hyper-awareness he knew couldn't last. "There was a better way," he said.

"What?"

"You." Tavin met her eyes boldly. Even beneath the shadow of the trees, her hair glinted with red highlights. Her pale skin shone like ivory. He dared to touch her cheek.

Aria bit her lip, pulling away. "You took a chance. I'm not what you think. I grew up with all the same stories my brother did."

The hair on Tavin's neck stood up; he ignored the feeling and made himself smile instead. After all, she'd rescued him from hell. "What stories?"

"About the Unmaker, the most powerful human mage of all."

"What happened?" Tavin finished off the flask and wiped his mouth. He shook the flask, wishing there was more. Aria didn't notice. She drew her knees up beneath her chin.

"Four hundred years ago in Etheria, the Unmaker found a place called the Pool of Chaos," she said. "It's sacred. Most people die when they touch the water, but instead it gave him great power. He was only a boy when it happened. Like you. Anything he wanted he could have … and it twisted him." She looked away, staring off into the rainy night. "In the end," she said, "he grew too powerful to stand against. The clans of Etheria surrendered to him in exchange for their lives, but it didn't make any difference. He went mad and became worse than cruel. He killed thousands of us."

She trailed off. "No one has trusted a human since," she said finally. "I've always been told that humans are empty inside. My people believe that it was this emptiness that drove the Unmaker mad."

Tavin's stomach turned.

"Except for you," he said. "You don't believe that."

Aria paused. She turned her head so her hair fell across her face like a veil. "Of course not," she answered. "I mean, not about you anyways. But … I'm not kind or good, Tavin, if that's what you think. I'm just done with being a princess locked in her tower."

She stretched and climbed to her feet.

"What about your brother?" Tavin asked.

Aria's eyes glowed green with anger. "He's sick," she said. "Like the Unmaker. He's been rotting from the inside out for years and I'm the only one in this whole cursed kingdom to see it." Her lips twisted. She rose to her feet. "With Mya's help, they won't discover your escape until dawn. Now, do you want to get that book or not?"

"The Black Sword Awakes"

Aria held the torch aloft. The light flickered off a narrow spiraling staircase, and illuminated three arched doorways. Tavin looked back at the staircase, surprised he'd made it down without cracking his skull open.

The stair began beneath the stage at the front of the cathedral and plunged straight down. With the pale light of the church's silver globe nothing but a pinprick above him, Tavin felt as if he stood upon the threshold of a cold and dark hell.

"This is the entrance to the catacombs," Aria said. "The book is this way."

She took the middle passageway. It continued to sink into the earth until it emerged into a cavern so large that the light of Aria's torch couldn't touch the far end.

Stalactites dripped from the ceiling, and round pools of shimmering green water gleamed with thick crystal formations. Tavin wrinkled his nose; the air was cold and smelled like gas.

Aria balanced upon the slippery rock and ran lightly down a narrow path between the green pools. Tavin covered his nose against the petroleum stench in the water. He moved gingerly forward, one hand pressed against the fresh bandages across his side. The fiery drink he'd had coursed through his brain, numbing his pain and making him feel curiously light-headed. Despite Aria's ministrations, he moved like an old man in need of a walker.

In the middle of the cavern, they came to a small island formed of crystal. Plunged into a high mound of rock was a sword, the blade as black as the hilt. A silver star shone in its pommel and it pulsed with faint purple light. Pinned to the rock, with the sword driven though it, was a thick leather-bound book.

Tavin stopped dead in his tracks, his pulse turning up a notch. The sight of the sword affected him like a vision of his own death. It terrified him and entranced him at the same time. He knew he should turn around and leave, but he felt inexplicably drawn to the sword.

Aria squinted against the purple light as if it hurt her eyes, and circled cat-like around the mound.

She read the expression on Tavin's face with an ironic smile.

"You want to touch it, don't you?" she said. "It makes me feel like running away as fast as I can."

"What is it?" Tavin couldn't stop staring.

"The sword of Nod, Queen of the Underworld. Or at least it used to be. A long time ago, the sword was stolen from her for another purpose."

"What?" Purple light rippled across the black blade like water. Tavin's hands began to tremble.

"That sword is what defeated the Unmaker. It was a human who did it." Aria dropped a hand gently across the back of Tavin's neck; her fingers lay like cold tentacles against his skin. "The silver star in the pommel binds the dark magic of the sword and unites it to human mages. Only a human can pull the sword from that rock and as far as we know, it's impossible to destroy. Trust me, we've tried."

Tavin's hands itched. Forgetting his injuries, he stood taller. Somehow, he knew the sword hilt would fit perfectly into his palm.

"It was placed in the stone to guard the book." Aria gave him a playful shove. "Well, what are you waiting for?"

Tavin wasn't sure.

He took half a step forward and suddenly recalled the oracle Lucy had spoken to him. It seemed like years ago. "The black sword awakes ..." He said the words under his breath. It didn't feel right. His need for the sword was simply too strong. Was it truly destiny, he wondered, or was it something more sinister?

Aria spoke into his ear. "You're the one who's supposed to pull

out the sword and retrieve the book, Tavin. Ever since I saw your scar
I knew it was true."

Tavin felt his will falter. All he wanted — all he ever needed was
right before him, literally in his grasp. He opened a sweaty palm.
"This is to help my sister, right?" Tavin asked. "I mean, that's why
we're here?"

Aria's eyes narrowed with impatience. "Of course. Just pull out
the sword and you'll have more power than anyone's ever dreamed."

"And you'll have the book." He said the words with a growing
sense of dread.

"And I'll have the book," she repeated. "What are you waiting for?"

Tavin's head began to throb. His doubts found more words. "Do
you love me?" he asked.

Aria cocked her head, a black smile widening across her lips.
"Sure."

Tavin's heart sank. "What will you do with the book? I mean,
once you've got its power?"

Aria tapped her foot. "Why should you care? You've seen how
things are here," she said. "I'm going to change the world," she said.
"I'm going to bring new life to this place and get rid of the ones that
are killing us — like the Chill and the Goblins. You've seen what
they're like."

Tavin's skin grew clammy, his mouth dry. "Someone tried that
once in my world," he said. "A lot of innocent people died. What
gives you the right to decide something like that?"

Aria's eyes narrowed. "What's the matter with you? I know you want the sword. As to my right, in case you missed it, I was born with it." She crossed her arms. "Don't you trust me?"

The sound of dry laughter echoed through the cavern. Tavin turned slowly around, feeling as if he were pulling against an invisible tide. Orange light oozed towards them. It flared and turned the green water on the floor to a muddy brown color. For the first time, Tavin noticed rectangular holes set at intervals into the cavern walls. A golden gleam moved among the shadows.

A bubble of anger rose in Tavin's brain. The red-eyed prince emerged from the passageway on large orange wings and landed upon the narrow path. His gaze swept the wide cavern, a haughty expression upon his face.

Aria's free hand sparked like an electric short. "Tavin," she said. "Pull out the sword."

Prince Axim laughed again—the sound rolling across the cavern like a low ringing bell. "She's lying to you. It's never been about changing the world. It's always been about power."

"Tavin," Aria said, "save your sister. Get me that book."

A cold sweat broke out across Tavin's forehead. He wanted to grab the blade and rush out of there but he could no longer ignore the ache in his heart. He looked at Aria and for the first time since they'd met — he saw her.

"It appears your obsession has led us into dangerous waters, dear sister," Prince Axim jeered. "Befriending a human? You are desperate indeed."

Tavin took a careful heart-breaking step back from Aria.

"He's right," he said, so softly only she could hear it. "You only care about power."

Axim snapped his fingers. With the clink of drawn weapons, guards with golden breastplates and helmets rushed from the deep recesses in the cavern walls. Each guard bore the red-eye insignia upon their right shoulder. Their mirror-polished armor filled the dank cavern with dull yellow light.

Aria turned her back to Tavin. "Axim, you worm," she said, her voice low and brittle. "You've been waiting for this your entire life, haven't you?"

The corner of Axim's mouth climbed up into a smirk. "Things have changed while you were gone, sister. It's a pity you missed my Initiation. Father said I endured the ritual better than any mage he'd seen."

Aria barked out a laugh. "You think I care if they call you a mage or not? I don't need a ritual to beat you, and I don't need a book. We both know it."

Axim's cheeks reddened with anger. "It's against nature for girls to do magic."

Aria's eyes flickered with triumph. "Don't you have a single thought in your fat head that someone else didn't put there?" she demanded. She flung the torch she carried into the water, igniting its oily surface. The flame spread. It raced along the cannels that crisscrossed the cavern, higher than Tavin's head and flickering with blue and green at its tips.

Axim faltered. "You'll never be a real mage."

Aria tensed and turned her head slightly towards Tavin. "You're useless," she said tersely. "Now get out of here before I kill you myself."

Aria's wings snapped into action. In a swift arc, she pulled a glowing sword from the air and exploded towards Axim like a small rocket. Axim screamed and jumped back. Aria missed but made up for it by kicking Axim in the face as she shot towards the ceiling.

The guards moved in streaks of golden light towards their prince, leaving Tavin alone beyond the circle. Tavin froze, knowing that now was his chance to run, but unable to pick a direction. He gritted his teeth in frustration. Whatever she'd done, he wouldn't leave Aria.

"Hold!" Axim shouted, his nose swollen and leaking purple blood. He waved the guards back from the small island where he stood. "I want to take her down myself!"

Aria dropped from the ceiling like a streak of dark lightning. Axim pressed his palms outward, sending a wall of purple light blazing across her path. Aria's swords tore a hole through the wall with the sound of ripping fabric. With a taunting laugh, she slapped the flat of her blade along Axim's face, scorching a red welt across his cheekbone.

Axim's wings hummed angrily. Blood dripped down his chin and onto the collar of his fine cloak. He rose wrathfully into the air and began hurtling giant balls of black and purple lightning bolts. Aria, flew high and free, cutting Axim's magic to ribbons with a look of happy fury.

Axim flicked out his fingers and sent out streaks of crackling purple lightning, hiding them behind the storm balls. Aria dodged all but the last. The purple lightning strike hit her square in the chest and blasted her back against the far wall of the cavern.

Tavin yelled and ran forward into the lake, stupidly attracting the attention of the guards. He picked up stones and flung them at the prince, drawing a ripple of dull laughter from several of the fairies.

Axim's mouth soured. "Take care of him," he demanded.

Aria hung in the air, her body jerking as fingers of lightning coursed down her arms and legs. The blue swords in her hands flickered and dimmed.

Then she looked up, wiping a trickle of purple from the corner of her mouth. She smiled slightly. "So, you have been practicing."

Tavin couldn't help but cheer. He threw his fist in the air and flung more stones towards the fairies streaking towards him. Suddenly he made up his mind and turned back towards the black sword.

Brother and sister flew to the ground, landing on a second small island amidst the flaming water, encircled by a ring of golden guards.

The instant his feet touched down, Axim hurled handfuls of lightning towards Aria. Aria's blades spun in blurry circles, deflecting the magic back at him. Axim thrust out a wall to save himself from his own bolts.

Tavin scrambled from the water and up the rocky mound. Just being close to the black sword made him feel stronger. His arms and legs didn't seem so stiff. He hardly even noticed the wound in his side.

"Energy bolts," Aria scoffed. "You won't get me twice with those."

Aria brought her hands together joining her blades into one

large sword that pulsed with power. She swung it over her head and smashed it down into the cavern floor.

The cavern floor rippled like water, moving outward from Aria in expanding rings towards Axim. Then the rings burst, expelling stone and earth, and blasting Axim through the flames and into the water.

The shock wave knocked Tavin to his knees; his hands scraped across rock. A heavy golden sword shattered the rock near his shoulder, sending flying shards towards his face. Tavin threw his hands up and rolled.

Aria ran towards the place where Axim spluttered and smoldered, his scorched robes dragging behind him as he clawed out of the water. She backed up quickly, her eyes bright and hard.

Axim drew himself straight, his red eyes glowing. "You'll pay for this," he said. He made two fists, but the crackle of lightning never left his hands. Instead, it arched back on itself and struck him in the belly. Axim screamed and fell onto his back.

Aria dropped her hands triumphantly; her swords vanished. "Energy follows the path of water," she said. "You try your lightning trick on me again and you'll just make it worse. Admit it, brother, you're beaten."

A weight like a hundred bricks drove into Tavin's back and pounded him into the ground. Tavin felt his ribs crack and his lungs compress as the air exploded out of him.

Axim struggled to his feet, looking like a drowned rat. "Take her!" he screamed.

The royal guard dropped like vengeful angels. Aria hardly had time to form her swords before they fell upon her.

Black mist flowed out of the sword and towards Tavin. He reached an arm forward. A heavy hand closed about his wrist and hauled him to his knees.

Aria struggled on the ground with her ankles bound and her wrists tied behind her. Nearly twenty guards limped back to make a space for Axim to approach.

Axim walked cautiously towards his sister. His face, no longer enraged, was calculating. He held a handkerchief delicately to the wound on his cheek. "You're right," he said softly. "I admit it, you beat me fair and square. Your magic packs a punch; I'm just glad I had the chance to see the threat in time."

Axim reached into his sodden robes and pulled out a milky white stone, the size of an egg, hung on the end of a silver chain.

Aria's eyes widened.

"Measures must be taken" Axim continued, "for everyone's safety, including yours."

"That belongs to father," Aria said. Her voice shook unsteadily. "He would have never given it to you freely. Axim, what have you done?"

"The king has taken ill," Axim replied. "It happened suddenly in the night. A maid saw the human leave his chambers." Axim showed his fangs. "Mother's caring for him, leaving me in charge." He dangled the stone before Aria's face. "He'll never miss it."

"Traitor," Aria hissed. She tugged furiously upon the ropes about her wrists. "You planned this."

Axim knelt down. "You've never seen a wish rock this big up close, have you? I've often wondered what it would do to you. The little ones fill up so quickly ... do you think this one has enough room for all your magic?" Axim's face twisted to a look of pure evil. "I do."

With a movement like the strike of a snake, Axim's arm shot out. He pressed the stone down against Aria's forehead. The stone flashed white. Aria screamed, the sound thrown from one wall of the cavern to the other, lingering even after she fell unconscious.

Axim pulled the stone away. It made a hissing noise and left a round wound in the middle of Aria's forehead. He pressed two pale fingers against her throat.

"She'll live," he said. "Untie the princess and take her to her quarters. She's no longer a threat." Axim's eyes raised and fixed on Tavin. "Kill the human."

Tavin's scar burned. Purple fire pulsed down the length of the black sword in sync with the beat of his heart. In his mind, Tavin reached for the fire, yearning to touch the sword. The black mist that streamed from the sword twisted about his arm. As if responding to his call, purple flames exploded outwards in waves of searing heat from the blade. Tavin's captors yelled and fell back. Tavin climbed to his feet and stumbled forward. He no longer remembered pain or weariness. His fingers closed around the hilt of the black sword like meeting the grasp of an old friend.

The black sword slid easily from the stone. Tavin lunged and caught the book pinned beneath the blade, thrusting it under the waist belt of his jeans. His arms swung upward, clashing against a guard's blade in a two-handed parry. The force of the guard's attack drove Tavin to his knees. Then, with a shudder, the black sword cut through the fairy's yellow weapon, and sliced deep into the metal of the guard's breastplate.

Tavin jumped forward, his blade wet with fairy blood. His hands shook. He had no way of knowing if the guard at his feet was dead or not. Another guard spun towards him, twisting through the air like a drill bit. Tavin dodged and brought the black sword down, slicing the guard's wings from his back.

The prince screamed. "Impossible!" he said. He hissed through his teeth. "The weapons of the royal guard don't break!"

The sword sang through his mind. Tavin could feel it pulse with dark and happy vibrations. Tavin slid into a pool of green water and dove beneath the flames. He emerged close to the prince. A purple streak of lightning hissed towards him. Tavin snapped the sword partway up but only deflected part of the bolt. The rest blew him into the water.

Moments later, he opened his eyes, floating face down. His ears rang. His grip on the sword was a dead man's grip. He couldn't have let go if he'd wanted to. His feet found the ground and he pushed himself up.

The prince stood on shore. His leer changed to a look of shock as Tavin sprang for him. He tried to run, but tripped on his long royal robes and fell flat instead.

Tavin was on him in an instant. He pushed him over and dug the sword into the baby fat beneath the prince's chin. Every moment of fear, humiliation, capture, and torture flooded into Tavin's mind as he stared into Axim's ruby eyes. The prince looked back at him with an equal measure of hatred.

"Cut her free," Tavin hardly recognized his own voice. His hands still trembled, making a jagged scratch in the prince's neck.

Axim's lips curled.

"Don't," Tavin said. The weakness in his voice conveyed far more than an angry threat. "Don't test me."

"Free her." Axim said. He looked at Tavin with loathing. "You'll pay for this, human. This means war."

A guard carried Aria's limp form and laid her by Tavin's feet. Tavin turned the prince towards the wall, and after the guard backed away, pulled the spell book free.

"You all know what this is?" he asked. "I've heard it holds the secrets of centuries of magic. It'll make anyone who possesses it immensely powerful." He'd caught their attention. Every eye turned towards the book.

"Don't," Axim snarled. "They're just peasants."

The book grew warm in Tavin's hand. It began to glow with a soft yellow light. "This book can make all your dreams come true," he yelled. "Everything you ever wanted or desired. It can heal all your diseases; make all your problems disappear!"

Tavin hurled the book towards the far wall of the cavern, where the oily flames burned the highest. The pages caught on fire even as it passed through the air. A shout of alarm went up around the cavern.

The fairy guards rushed towards the book in a bloody fray. Many hands clutched desperately at the torn pages, even as they burned.

Tavin scooped Aria up in his arms and dashed for the passageway. At his back, the book, slick with oil, smoked and charred to ash, crumbled towards the bottom of the pool.

Tavin reached the passage. Near the opening to the cavern, a long stalactite hung nearly to the floor. Struck with inspiration, Tavin shifted Aria's weight to one side, flipped the grip on his sword and swung backhanded at the rock. The magical sword buried itself deep and slid cleanly out, sparking with light. Tavin didn't wait to see what happened next. He ran for all he was worth. Falling stone groaned and smashed to the ground, sealing the way behind him.

Banished

Tavin lay Aria gently down upon the wet grass. The rain had stopped and the soft glow of glossymer lit the sky above them.

He stroked her hair. The first time he'd seen her, every inch of her had sparked with life. Now she looked plain and tired — almost human. The mark on her forehead remained raw and bloody. Her hair spread upon the grass like black coal; the red highlights were gone. When she opened her eyes, they were the flat green color of the stormy ocean. He jerked his hand back.

"You shone back there," she said. "I saw you." It almost sounded like an accusation.

"I don't know if you should talk," he replied.

Aria shook her head. "You don't know what you looked like. Your eyes …" She trailed off and reached a hand towards his face.

"There was fire in your chest," she said. Tavin turned away.

Aria lay still for a moment, breathing low and shallow. She watched him the way an animal would, trying to read his expression. Tavin felt his face grow hard.

"Don't you dare judge me," she said at last. "You don't know what it's been like."

Tavin remained silent.

"All my life I've been forced to hold back," she said, "deny what I really am. Fairies don't have girl mages, so ever since I built my first light ray they've been trying to 'cure' me."

"Quiet," Tavin pushed her against the ground. "Lie still."

"My father decided I was dangerous," Aria continued, her voice empty of emotion. "He gave my servants and guards special privileges. He allowed them to use force to control my 'fits' and try to bind my magic." Her lips tightened. "It's why I ran away, but you can never run away from who you are." She gave Tavin an odd look. "I'm not beaten, you know. The secrets in the book will teach me how to control my power, and it'll make me stronger. It will show me how to recover my magic." Aria's voice grew horse with passion. "I'll challenge the mages," she said. "Open the Gates. My people won't have to stay stuck on a dying world; magic can heal and give hope back to your world. Don't you understand? We won't be alone anymore."

"What about my sister?" Tavin's worlds fell heavy upon his tongue. What did he care about kingdoms, when she was dying? "Was there any truth to that book being able to cure her?'

Aria stared boldly into his eyes. "Don't be so small minded." She flashed her fangs and grabbed the collar of his jacket. She pressed her mouth hard against his, hungry and violent.

Tavin wrenched away, wiping a bloody lip with the back of his hand. He felt the darkness press against his mind once again. "The book's gone," he said. "I watched it burn."

Aria slapped him across the face. "Liar."

Tavin rubbed his cheek, his stomach knotting with pain. She'd used him. She'd taken his need and manipulated it to get what she wanted. His knuckles whitened in anger. "I don't know what it was we had," he said, "but it's over."

Aria rolled towards the ground and screamed. She tore up handfuls of grass and dug her fingers into the earth. She curled up as if in pain and buried her head into her arms. Finally, she lapsed into dark silence.

A few minutes passed. Tavin began to wonder if she was still conscious.

Then she spoke, her voice cold and empty of emotion. "Leave me. I'd rather die than live without magic. Flesh is weak."

For a moment, Tavin was tempted. "Well, princess," he said. "I guess you'd better get used to it." He slid the black sword through a belt loop and gathered her into his arms. He scanned the dark line of trees and picked out a path he hoped led in the right direction. "And don't test me. If you bite me again, I'll drop you in the first swamp I find."

Tavin walked swiftly downhill, leaving the glowing trees behind. Even though he no longer held the black sword, he could still feel it feed him strength and comfort as it brushed against his thigh. The wound in his side had become nothing more than another ragged scar. The bruises on his face no longer pained him and if his nose seemed slightly off center from where it once was, he figured he was lucky that it still worked at all.

The ground grew spongy and wet, soaking through his high tops and dragging heavily on his jeans. Tavin didn't want to even think about what his feet would smell like when he pulled his shoes off. It probably wouldn't be much different from the smell of rot that tainted the air around him.

The trees turned crooked and rubbery, and swampweed tangled his path. It became harder and harder to progress forward. Tavin found himself switching directions several times to avoid the shallow bogs that barred his way.

Aria said nothing. She laid still, her head tucked against his shoulder. Tavin checked occasionally to see if she remained conscious. A dull ache that he didn't want to admit grew in his heart. He felt the place she'd bit him with his tongue, tasting the blood.

The swamp remained as empty as a graveyard. The many trees and soggy pools made it hard to travel in a straight direction. The deeper into the swamp he traveled, the greater Tavin's sense of unease grew. Once again he felt as if something were watching him, hovering beyond the edge of his sight and whispering his name in the dark.

Tavin thought he caught a glimpse of a tall figure sliding through the gloom, but when he looked a second time, he saw no one. He picked up his pace. He didn't care which direction he headed, he just wanted to escape the swamp. Anywhere else would be better.

Tavin found a run of clear, even ground and broke into a light jog. The clouds broke overhead. Cold starlight drenched the ground in silvery light, gleaming off a line of ghostly grey that hung among the trees. Tavin dug his heels into the soft earth with an exclamation. A strand of webbing, as thick as his wrist, stretched tightly across his path.

Tavin dropped Aria upon the ground and freed his sword. He knew it would be useless to run. A giant web barred the way back, its strands still dripping. A shadow bent the branches overhead.

"What's happening?" Aria said.

The monster's song began before Tavin could answer.

> *Slippery little cheats,*
> *Make sweet meats*
> *They cut us and they break us*
> *But never will escape us.*

"Caveat," Aria shivered and exhaled a frosty breath. "She wouldn't dare. Not on our land. The king's guard will have her head."

A long high cackle dropped towards them. Madame Caveat flew from the treetops and landed like a ghost upon the leaf-strewn forest floor. She tucked her legs behind her back and spat through her grinning black teeth.

"The king was bitten by a wee little spider," Madame Caveat picked her teeth with a splinter of bone. "He lies so still tonight. He sleeps so deep. Perhaps he will never wake up!"

Tavin raised the sword. It flared alight with purple fire.

"What a pretty toy!" Caveat cackled. "Do you know how it works?" Caveat's jaw unhinged and a ball of webbing flew towards him. Tavin tightened his grip on the blade. Its edge passed cleanly through the webbing. He jumped to the side and rolled. Caveat sprang into the air, her legs unfolding and her talons dripping with poison.

The black sword moved of its own accord, twisting in a blurry circle. Caveat swung on a line above Tavin's head. Adrenaline pounding in his veins, Tavin rolled to his feet and chased after her. Caveat clawed her way up a tree. Tavin felt a thrill course through him. The sword in his hand pulsed with life of its own.

"Tavin, no!" Aria said. "It's a trap!"

The ground dropped away beneath him, vanishing as if it'd never existed. Sucking mud pulled him downwards.

"Stay calm," Aria cried. "You can swim out if you stay calm!"

Something heavy slammed him under. Tavin's throat filled with mud and the sword was wrenched from his grasp. Tavin's feet found the bottom and he pushed up.

Aria screamed. The weight forced him under again. Tavin thrashed, fighting furiously. He grabbed hold of what felt like a long hairy leg. A second later, webbing encased his arm.

Tavin broke the surface. "Give it back!" he yelled. "It's mine!"

Madame Caveat yanked him up onto shore with a sticky strand. She hauled him from the swamp like a dog drags a stick, cackling in triumph.

"So careless, little hero! The master says you mustn't die. But he says nothing about your nasty toys."

Tavin fought back with all he had, clawing his way to his knees and tackling Madame Caveat around the waist. She rolled over onto her back, her legs waving in the air like a dying insect.

"What master?" he growled. "Is it Axim? How did he know where to find us?"

Caveat shrieked with laughter and bit him with her rotten teeth. Tavin clung fast to her middle, just beyond the reach of Madame Caveat's poisoned talons. He threw his head forward smashing her in the mouth. He felt a tooth dig into his scalp as he raised his head and hit her again. Madame Caveat spat mucus into his face and kneed him in the groin with her human leg.

Tavin jerked his legs up, his eyes streaming with tears. He head-butted her once more before rolling free. Expecting to feel a poisoned talon any second, Tavin scrabbled in the dirt and found a short pointed stick, but when he jumped to his feet, his enemy was gone.

She crouched several feet away in the lee of a crooked tree, holding her jaw. She hissed curses at him through her broken mouth, her black eyes sparking hate. Aria pulled herself into the cover of a low bush, still too weak to stand, much less fight. She watched the fight with wide eyes. Tavin tightened his hold on the stubby stick. It would end tonight, he decided. Aria would never be afraid of Caveat again.

A whistling noise passed through the air and three arrows, like shafts of moonlight, landed in a row across Caveat's path.

Caveat hissed and spat, retreating further back into the shadows. "Curses upon you and blight upon your family, king of the forest! This is none of your concern!"

Three figures burst from the trees, glowing with soft silver light. One was a giant stag with a mighty rack of ebony antlers and a thick collar of fur. Beside him, there stood a boy and girl. Both were pale and tall with fine regal features. Tavin recognized the boy as Prince Whelin. The girl held a bow and arrow. Her long white hair hung loosely to her waist. She looked younger than Tavin, yet her eyes were as old as the hollow places deep beneath the mountains.

The stag was heavier and much larger than a horse. His face was noble and wise. Of the three of them, he cast the brightest light.

"Be gone!" the stag bellowed.

"You are banished from these lands," cried the prince. "Monster of the night, to challenge us is to invite death!"

The large stag spoke to the girl with the bow. "Be strong, my daughter."

She raised her bow, her eyes grim.

Madame Caveat knew a lost fight when she saw it. She fled, marking her trail with curses and poison.

Prince Whelin headed directly for Aria. At the sight of him, Aria burst into tears and buried herself into his waiting arms. Tavin's heart darkened with jealously.

Prince Whelin eased Aria from the bushes and lifted her out of the mud. He washed her face with water from a flask.

"You're safe now," Prince Whelin said. "We received your message and came as quickly as we could."

"It's become worse," Aria said. Her voice shook. "Caveat's poisoned my father and Axim helped. Axim's taken control. I don't know what's become of my mother."

Prince Whelin's face clouded with anger. He carried Aria over to the white-haired girl. "Feldora," he said, "take Aria to our home. Her heart is broken; she must have time to mend it." The girl nodded. In a flash of white light, she transformed into a slender doe. Prince Whelin gathered her bow and helped Aria onto Feldora's back.

The white stag caught Tavin's eye and stepped forward. "I am Ieda, Emperor of these lands," he said. "You've proven yourself brave. Your grandfather will be proud."

Tavin nodded and batted mud from his jacket. Aria rode away without a single look back. He ground his teeth. "It's gone," he said. "Caveat's taken my sword. I finally had something—something that mattered, that could help—and she stole it from me."

"The black sword wasn't yours to keep," Whelin said. He crossed his arms. "It belongs to Guardians: those who fight and die to protect the peace. It is not a tool to be used for personal gain."

"My sister is dying!" Tavin yelled.

Whelin's brow furrowed. "And Princess Aria almost died as well. Who else will you sacrifice to get what you want?"

Tavin's hands turned white with fury. "I've been beaten, attacked, and betrayed, all on the slimmest hope that I may save Moreanna. I'll do what I have to."

"Tavin," Whelin spoke heavily, "your sister …"

"You!" Tavin jabbed a finger towards the prince. "You have the gift of healing and you won't even try."

That shut the prince up. His eyes widened.

The Emperor stamped his hoof. "Enough! You speak of things you don't understand. I am pained to hear about your sister, but our world stands on the brink of war. Now all of Etheria will rumble with talk of a human spy. Go! My son will show you the way. Your presence here tips the balance in a struggle we cannot afford to lose."

Tavin clenched his teeth. "It'd be better if your world never even existed," he said.

Whelin looked up sharply, his eyes hard and black. "We have heard those evil words before. It is time to leave, Tavin. Leave Etheria, and leave your grandparents to guard their secrets. If you value your life, you won't return."

The Cost

*T*he morning smelt like ash; the air had none of its usual crispness. Tavin lay upon his bed, staring out through the glass balcony door at the white morning sky.

He pressed his hand over his scar, at the place where it intersected with his heart. It ached, and there was nothing he could do to ease the pain.

Never trust a fairy.

He'd lost. He'd failed to find a cure.

He'd lost the sword and he'd lost — her.

He rose and padded barefoot to the wardrobe. He chose a shirt and yanked it on. He even fished a comb and some gel from his duffle bag. Peering into the small mirror on the back of the wardrobe door, he parted his hair to the side, reminding himself of his father as he did so. Tavin gaped at his reflection. With clean clothes and a shower, he almost looked like a normal teenager. He fingered the new crooked bend in his nose. Well, almost normal.

Tavin collapsed to the floor, his sides shaking, his eyes raw with tears that wouldn't come. He wished he'd never come here. The Shadowlands had done nothing but rip open old wounds and dig into him with fresh ones. In the beginning, it had seemed to offer hope, holding the promise of a magical cure like a dangling carrot in front of his nose. He'd believed it because Moreanna believed it. She'd been so sure the answer to her sickness was here. She'd never been wrong before.

That thought was a dangerous one. Even after all that had happened, it teased Tavin with hope he knew wasn't there. A muscle in his jaw flexed. Moreanna was wrong this time, that was all there was to it. She was wrong and he was …

… broken.

Something brushed against his foot. Tavin jerked in surprise. "Pip!" He picked up the scrawny rat and cradled him against his chest. Again, his eyes grew sore. He ran a finger lightly along the rat's spine, scratching him behind his ears, wondering at the simple, unconditional love of animals. Aria had called him the defender of the ugly, and that was true, but in that moment, Tavin realized just how much he needed them as well.

A knock sounded on the door, Tavin didn't even bother to rise. "Come in."

Opa walked through, carrying a brown paper package beneath his arm. He settled into the chair by Tavin's bed.

"So it's true." Opa nodded towards the sloppy packing job Tavin had begun. "You are leaving today."

Tavin nodded, his eyes sliding away from Opa's gaze. Opa smelt like warm earth and rain. His eyes were the color of a perfect summer day.

"It's for the best," Opa continued. "This place is no longer safe for children. I will write you when things are better."

Tavin didn't know what to say. Opa's words only made him feel worse, as if he were a puppy dog being sent to slink back to its kennel after doing something wrong.

Pip scampered down Tavin's arm and climbed into Opa's lap. Opa laughed. "I was saving this for later." He pulled a napkin wrapped around a piece of cheese and a slice of bread from his pocket. "Your friend is quite the scavenger."

Tavin nodded numbly. "Can you take care of him for me?"

Opa clicked his tongue. "If he minds his manners, he will live very well while you are gone. But he should know to stay out of Oma's kitchen. I cannot protect him if he goes there."

"Do you hear that, Pip?" Tavin stood and rummaged for his jacket. He'd thrown his clothes in the laundry, but no amount of washing could repair the many rips and stains the jacket had endured.

"One moment, Tavin," Opa left the room and returned with a long dark brown jacket. "Take mine."

"You don't have to — "

"I wish it. I have others." Opa held the jacket out and helped Tavin put it on. "There, what a handsome look! Such a thing doesn't ever go out of style! And you even have room to grow!"

A lot of room. The jacket almost touched the floor. Looking up at Opa, Tavin wondered if he'd ever be tall enough. The jacket made him feel a bit like he was wearing a dress.

"It's awesome," he said. "Everybody at home will want to know where I found it." Tavin smiled at his own joke and tugged on the shoulders. The warm smell of spices and laundry soap lingered on the material. It seemed Oma's touch got into everything. He supposed the split up the back wasn't too bad. The jacket made him feel like a cowboy, or maybe a desperado outlaw.

He looked at his old army jacket, discarded on the floor. "My dad gave me that one," he said, a small lump in his throat. "I guess it's only appropriate that it looks like that in the end."

Opa grabbed him, drawing him close and burying Tavin in a hug. "Hush, hush, my boy, do not say such things. Those words can turn your heart to poison."

Tavin gave Opa a tight squeeze before pulling away. Opa, with a smile, held out the brown parcel.

"Another gift. I found it in the garden this morning."

Tavin took the package. It smelled of blackberries and lavender.

Strong bold letters spelled his name out across the top. Inside he found a pair of orange wings and a note.

'Meet me at the ruins. —A'

"Perhaps your friend wishes a last goodbye?" Opa wiggled his eyebrows.

Tavin silently cursed the traitorous thoughts that rushed through his mind. He wished the note didn't change things, but his racing heart told him otherwise. He wanted to hold her before he left. Just one last time.

"Do you need a ride into town?" Opa watched Tavin's conflicting expressions with amusement.

"Um, yes."

"I will meet you by the barn at two."

"Sure. Two … sounds good."

Tavin hardly heard him. He'd already slipped his arms through the thin straps and opened the balcony door. He turned his face up towards the sky, and opened his wings to the warm air currents spinning playfully about the house. Opa smiled and shuffled from the room, carefully closing the door behind him.

Aria perched upon the edge of the crumbling wall, her legs dangling into open space. Despite the mildness of the afternoon, she wore dark leggings, a black hood, and a long grey scarf. Her wings had no color in them at all. They oscillated gently behind her, appearing like the flash of sunlight on water.

She didn't move until he landed nearly on top of her, even though she'd seen him approach. She watched him with the glassy gaze of a dead fish.

"Nice jacket," she said. He couldn't tell if she meant it or not.

"I got your message." He sat next to her. Close enough to touch but not too close. The humid afternoon draped the rolling fields beneath them in a murky veil. "What do you want?"

She tried a smile. "Your nose has a new look as well," she said. "I like it. It makes you look like a dangerous vagabond."

Tavin bit back a smile and crossed his arms. He didn't want to make this too easy for her. "When are you going to get to the point where you say you're sorry? Or did you just bring me here to waste my time?"

Aria hesitated. Tavin thought he saw a tear and immediately felt remorse. He was starting to wonder if he was supposed to apologize after all, when she spoke again.

"They tried," she said. Aria fidgeted with her scarf. "They tried to bring my magic back but nothing worked. It's gone like it was never there." A round pale scar on her forehead caught the light. It glimmered like a pearl. Her fingers tore clover from the rocks. "It's stupid, isn't it? All I can think about is magic and you don't even want it, but you have it and I ..." she trailed off, her hands balled tightly. "I guess I have to accept what I am now."

Somehow, Tavin doubted she would. He looked off into the

distance. The sky was pale and featureless, lacking even the smallest wrinkle of cloud

"I'm sorry," her voice was small. "I did use you — I thought you could help me. I didn't know what humans were like. I didn't know you could be kind or brave. I was taught that all humans are violent and selfish. I — I wanted to say that before you left; and that I really do want your sister to get better."

Tavin let out a slow breath. "I didn't want to hurt you," he said. "But I've seen humans mess things up so much on our side, I was afraid the same thing might happen on yours."

Slowly he reached out his hand and let it rest on top of hers. Aria squeezed his fingers and pulled back.

"No," she said softly.

Tavin's heart grew cold.

"What?"

Aria sighed. "Forget it. I just wanted to say sorry. I didn't come so we could fight."

"What is it?"

"I just want to be friends again," she returned.

Tavin turned towards her. "You're kidding me, right?"

Aria shook her head.

"Well, what's the problem?"

Aria met his eyes with a look somewhere between remorse and pity. "I'm to be with Whelin," she said. It's always been that way."

Tavin's mind overloaded with static noise. It took him a moment for him to register her words. "What?!"

"I'm promised."

He still couldn't believe it. "What do you mean?"

"I told you, I'm of age. I'm with Whelin. We're going to become one."

"As in marriage?"

She nodded. "As humans say, yes, like marriage."

"You're lying."

"I never meant for things to happen the way they did," she said. "I'm sorry. I thought I owed it to you to let you know face to face."

Tavin began to get angry again. "You owe me more than that. A lot more." The ache in his heart returned, only this time he felt like a steamroller had squashed it. "Why?"

"I love him," she said. "I know you don't see it, but I do. I always have. Ever since I was a little girl, he's taken care of me. Even when I tried to run away, he was there for me, waiting. You were — " she stumbled for her words. "I don't know what you were — more than I expected okay?" She flashed her fangs. "Not that I didn't enjoy it."

Tavin gritted his teeth. He wanted to hit her. "I don't know if you're even capable of love," he replied. He struggled to his feet. "I'm leaving," he opened his wings. "Don't worry. When you need me, I won't be there."

Aria opened her mouth to reply when a brilliant green flash filled the cloudless sky. The sound of thunder rumbled across the horizon. It came from the direction of his grandfather's farm. Tavin leaned forward, straining to see the village among the deepening shadows of late afternoon.

"What was that?"

"I don't know." Aria looked upset.

The wind blew hot against his face; it smelt sour. It smelt the way his house had the day his mother died.

Tavin didn't look at Aria. He couldn't. He jumped from the cliff, his heart racing. The wind buffeted and tore at his wings. It felt like a bad dream. The currents swooped low and viciously pulled him down with them. Aria flew behind, shouting directions. Tavin ignored her, struggling forward his own way.

He saw the old crooked tree on the hill near the farm. Then he saw the crater.

Tavin's throat closed with fear. Even from a distance, he could make out the unmoving figure lying in the heart of the crater.

"NO!" Tavin screamed. "NO!" He dropped into a sharp dive.

"Tavin!" Aria's voice was faint. "Tavin, the currents are unstable! You can't land there!"

With a choking noise, Tavin turned and landed in a rough stagger near the foot of the tree. He tore off his wings and raced towards the crater. All around its edges charred stalks of grain smoldered and burned. A fine sooty ash drifted like snow down from the sky.

Opa lay stretched out in the middle of the crater, his hands clawed and charred. The black raincoat he wore hung in ribbons.

Tavin fell down beside his grandfather.

"Tavin …" Opa's lips barely moved. His voice could have been the rustle of wind in the grass.

"Opa." Tavin buried his face in the tatters of his grandfather's coat. "Tell me who did this."

Opa's head moved slightly. "No." He reached up with his scared hand to touch Tavin's cheek. "I will die for them. I told you I would."

A sob broke from Tavin's throat.

Opa's eyes smiled. "Tavin ... Tavin ... my son."

Opa's hand slipped and fell.

Tavin's teeth ground together, biting back the scream that built inside. Opa's breath stilled, his unseeing eyes were wide and pale as the sky.

"Tavin ..." Aria stood close behind. "Tavin, is he ...?"

"Quiet!"

"Tavin — "

Tavin snarled. "Get out of here! Get out of my sight! NOW! I never want to see you again." Angry tears burned in Tavin's eyes. Aria jumped into the sky and streaked away, a black smudge of rage and sorrow against the grey.

Oma had heard the blast. At any other time the sight of Oma running with all her might, her perfectly pinned hair in wild shambles, would have been funny, but not today.

"Klause!" she screamed. "Klause!"

Tavin raked his fingers through the dirt. Anger made it hard for him to breathe. He gasped, choking through furious tears, reading the hateful words scratched into the dirt above Opa's head:

'He Broke the Rules.'

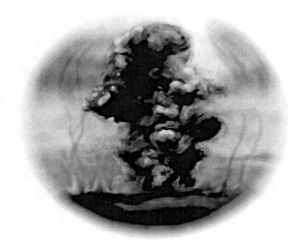

Smoke $\mathcal{A}$nd $\mathcal{A}$shes

Opa was dead.

Tavin didn't get a chance to speak with his grandmother. He'd heard her tell the attendants that Opa had been carrying an explosive to clear a blocked ditch. Then she'd left, riding the ambulance and clutching Opa's cold withered hand.

Opa was dead.

The police wanted to see the field. Tavin showed them where it was. The threat scrawled in the dirt had disappeared. He'd taken it all in numbly. He'd been unable to feel anything at all at first.

He told them he hadn't seen the explosion but had come running shortly afterwards. Talking helped; it was a way to hold back the grief. And the anger. He wanted to stay in control. He couldn't let himself fall apart, not again. An officer with a note pad nodded and strung yellow tape around the field.

Then he was alone.

Opa was dead.

The noise and the cries were gone. The busy neighbors had returned to their houses. The light faded and Tavin sat in the little kitchen, listening to the clock in the hall count out the seconds.

A phone rang causing him to jump.

"Hello?" asked a woman's voice. "Am I speaking to Mr. T. Thornbush?"

"Um," Tavin cleared his throat. "Uh, yes, I'm Tavin Thornbush."

"Tavin, my name is Adrienne; I'm from Child and Youth Crisis Relief Services. It is my understanding that you have recently been involved in a traumatic experience. I want you to know that this line is confidential and I'm here to help."

The lady sounded like she was reading a script.

"How do you know about me?"

"The reporting officer indicated in his initial reports that a minor was involved in the incident and was concerned that you may be in need of some extra guidance during this time."

"Thanks, but I'm okay." Tavin had never even heard of Child and Youth Crisis Relief Services.

"Tavin," said the voice. "It's not okay. You need to talk about this."

Tavin felt a hard lump build in his chest. It felt like anger.

"Tavin," said the voice again, "talk to me. How do you feel?"

Ice touched his heart. He embraced it.

"I'm going to kill them," he said.

She paused.

"That's good, Tavin, these feelings are natural, they need expression." The government lady cleared her throat. "Now who do you want to kill? Just let it out."

"Everyone." Tavin said the word like razor blades rubbing together.

"Tavin," she sounded worried. "Tavin. Your feelings are valid, but let's work together to put them into perspective. You are aware, of course, that what happened to your grandfather was a tragic accident? No one is to blame. Tavin? Are you still there? Tavin. I — I need you to stay on the line. I'm contacting a worker in your area to come and talk to you in person. Tavin?"

Tavin slammed the phone down so hard it ripped from the wall and crashed to the ground. He stalked angrily from the kitchen and to his bedroom. If they thought he was just going to tuck tail and return back home, they were wrong.

"Demetre!" he said. "Stop sulking and come out!"

The curtains across the balcony trembled slightly. Tavin went out onto the balcony. He squeezed his eyes shut, trying to envision a green light surrounding his hands.

"Come on, how does this work?" he said. He clenched his fists so hard his hands turned white, but nothing happened. Tavin swore.

He couldn't wait five or six months. If it took all night, he'd fig-ure out how to do what his grandfather had done. Then they'd pay. Their whole world would pay.

He dug into his pocket for his rubber band. Finding the pocket empty, he pulled a squashed cigarette carton from under his mattress and returned to the balcony.

"Screw them all," he said.

He flicked his lighter clumsily a few times. As he held the flame to his cigarette, a cold breeze brushed past him, pulling at the white curtains.

Tavin turned his head and saw something move inside his room.

Tavin took a draw on his cigarette, narrowing his eyes.

One of the rails on the balcony hung loose. Tavin twisted it around a few times and wrenched it free. Grinding the cigarette out on the concrete deck, he stood up and faced the open door to his room.

"Demetre? Come out. I need to talk to you."

Frosty silence answered him. Tavin thought of Caveat. He thought of Axim.

He walked boldly into the room.

Something moved to his left. Tavin turned and slammed the iron rail into the wardrobe, cracking the wood and dropping an avalanche of musky jackets.

Darkness flittered on the edge of his vision. Tavin swung blindly and buried the heavy rail into the wall.

He yanked the rail free and spun on the ball of his foot. He flipped the light switch. The light bulb hissed and died. Without missing a beat, Tavin opened his lighter and held the flame high.

A shadow moved, separating itself from the wall and forming a small, vaguely man-like shape.

Tavin's eyes widened as his lighter highlighted the flow of inky hair. A pale face watched him out of the darkness.

"You should have listened to me," Demetre's words rattled like bones. He looked like a withered old man.

"I know," Tavin said. "You were right, all along. You only tried to warn me."

"Why did you call me?" Demetre said. "I can't bring your grandfather back. All the magic in either world can't touch him now."

"Opa thought I had some special powers, and you said you were like me. If you can show me, I can finish this. I can make the human side safe again." Tavin boldly met Demetre's bottomless gaze. "You won't have to hide anymore."

Demetre threw his head back and laughed like a machine gun in a church. Screams hung in the silence he left behind.

"It will hurt," he said. "The power of a Guardian is not meant to be awakened so quickly."

"I don't care."

Demetre shrugged, something dark in his eyes. "My gift to you then," he said.

He changed shape; growing taller as his face retreated into a shadow that swallowed light.

Only his eyes remained visible, burning like red coals.

With a long pale hand, Demetre lifted Tavin by the front of his shirt and threw him across the room. Tavin's head and shoulder cracked against the plaster wall. He fell heavily upon his mattress, scrambling upright in confusion.

Warm fluid ran down the side of his head.

Demetre pounced on him, pinning him down onto the bed. Tavin swung the rail forward. Demetre caught it and wrenched it from his grasp. For a moment, Tavin saw Demetre's face flicker with the boyish features he'd abandoned.

"What are you?" Tavin said.

"Your future."

Heat passed from Demetre's hand and into his chest. Tavin began to shake, then to sweat. The heat grew and spasms racked his body. His eyes rolled back. Foam came from his mouth and ran down his cheeks.

Tavin fought against the fire that poured into his body: his hands in claws, his mouth wide with soundless screams. There was no escape. For an eternity, the flames burnt through him, consuming him with pain.

Then the fire cooled, rolling back on itself and settling in his stomach. Tavin became aware of the cool night air blowing across his face.

He opened his eyes.

He lay in his bed, sticky with sweat. Demetre floated above him, again in the form of a little boy, his body transparent.

The ghost opened his mouth and a thick column of black smoke poured out. He spoke.

"Let them burn."

Demetre vanished.

Tavin rose slowly and walked outside. The concrete balcony felt rough and cold beneath his feet. He pulled off his sweat-soaked shirt and saw a glimmer of light along the edges of his scar. The night air felt good upon his skin. Let them see the mark, he thought. Let them be afraid.

He slid the unfinished cigarette between his lips. He stretched his arms and drew in a slow breath. He was aware of every part of his body. Every piece felt stronger and more alive than ever before.

He raised his hand.

Like a flower opening, a small flame blossomed into the air. Tavin smiled, and drew more from the fire rolling in his belly. The floating white flame formed a sphere about the size of an orange. It flickered with flashes of color. Tavin passed the fire slowly from one hand to another, shivering in delight.

He was a mage.

The Cure

The greatest relief was that he didn't need to think anymore. For once, he knew exactly what he wanted to do. He wrapped his fingers around the edge of the balcony and jumped. He dropped like a panther and headed straight for the garden Gate.

A shadow rose before him, blocky and clumsy. It reached forward and its fingers lengthened into knives. Green magic cracked in a crown about its head.

Tavin rolled the cigarette between his teeth.

The golem's eyes were two hollows flickering green. It moaned and lifted an arm.

Tavin dropped to his belly. A bolt of green light passed over his head and singed the tree behind him. Tavin rolled to his knees. He built a fireball, spinning it between his fingers until it was the size of a soccer ball. The golem shot another ray. Tavin ran to the right.

Tavin's white fireball hit the golem in the chest and erupted like a small star. Long tongues of flame tore through the golem's shadow body in microseconds, ripping it to pieces. The golem, with a deep creaking moan, melted away.

Tavin walked forwards through falling ash — all that remained of the golem. He pressed his palm against the garden Gate, smiling grimly as it flickered to life with blue streaks of light. The runes above the door flashed.

"Tavin?"

A cold rush of air poured into the garden as the Gate swung open. Prince Whelin stood in the doorway, his pale skin glimmering against the dark fields behind him. He looked different from the haughty prince Tavin remembered — his hair was messy and he seemed tired.

Whelin walked warily into the garden. He moved through the long grass, stirring up the scent of wildflowers.

"Tavin," he said. "We need to talk."

Tavin recognized the look on Whelin's face. He laughed like a hollow drum and ground his cigarette into the dirt with his heel.

The prince was afraid.

"Tavin," Whelin said. "Something is happening; something very wrong."

Tavin wiped his mouth. "I'll say it is. My grandfather's dead."

Prince Whelin's eyes widened. "No."

"Your kind murdered my grandfather. He gave up everything to protect your world, and now he's dead."

"Tavin, you're not thinking clearly."

Tavin clenched his hands. "Actually, I think I finally understand what everyone has been saying this whole time. It's war, or didn't you know?"

"I'm trying to stop a war."

"Too late!" Tavin slapped his hands together. A river of white flame exploded from his fingers and roared towards the prince.

Whelin jumped onto the garden wall as the tree behind him burst into flames. Tavin clenched his jaw and flicked his wrists outwards, shooting fire hot enough to blacken and crack the stones beneath Whelin's feet.

"Your grandfather wouldn't want this!" Whelin said.

"Who cares?" yelled Tavin. "He's dead! I'm sure he didn't want that either!"

Whelin jumped towards him, spinning through the air. Tavin blocked with a wall of fire, but Whelin passed through only lightly singed.

Whelin's fist cut hard against Tavin's ear, throwing him backwards. Tavin drew a breath to spit flames, but another punch slammed into his belly, knocking the wind out of him.

Tavin crawled away, enraged. His fingers found a large stone. He turned, swinging the rock into Whelin's perfect face. Tavin felt flesh give and bone break beneath his blow with a wet cracking noise.

Whelin's fingers closed around Tavin's wrist in a vice grip. Tavin dropped the rock and hit the prince with a fiery left. The glancing blow smashed into Whelin's broken nose, distracting him long enough for Tavin to fill his lungs with air.

A sharp pain cut deep into Tavin's shoulder, paralyzing him in a flash of deathly cold. Tavin's fire froze in his chest. He crumpled backwards to the ground.

Whelin rocked back on his heels with a ragged breath, his face a pulpy mess. Tavin lay paralyzed on the grass in front of him, his eyes raging — Whelin's silver knife buried in his shoulder.

"I took away your gravechill," Whelin said. "I can give it back."

Killing cold gripped Tavin's limbs. He watched Whelin with bottled rage, his tongue a stone.

Prince Whelin climbed unsteadily to his feet. He walked away from Tavin's line of vision. He returned with a bucket of water and a rag. He cleaned the blood from Tavin's split lip, and then began washing his own face. As the blood and dirt came off, Tavin saw that the prince was healing. Whelin cracked his nose back into place and the purple swelling disappeared, leaving the prince unmarked.

Whelin looked down at him with cool amusement. "What did you think would happen?" he said. "That in your first mage fight you could take on a prince?"

Whelin closed his eyes. "This isn't you, Tavin."

Deep inside Tavin could feel the smallest spark burning. He focused on it, willing it to life.

The prince reached forward and pulled the blade up a little. The pain was excruciating. Tavin felt his tongue loosen.

"Tavin," Whelin said. "You might not understand this, but your grandfather made a choice to protect our world. He knew the danger, but he chose to help despite it. He took a risk, hoping he could heal an old wound."

Tavin felt his power begin to grow by degrees. His right arm began to tingle. "Why should I care?" he asked.

"Because you have a chance to make sure that what he fought for isn't lost." Whelin watched Tavin with concern. "If indeed the wound has not already cut you too deep."

A bead of sweat rolled down Tavin's forehead. The fingers on his right hand twitched with life. Whelin didn't seem to notice.

"Shut up," Tavin said. "I don't need a sermon from you." He reached over and yanked the silver blade from his shoulder. Fire burned through his veins faster than thought. He leapt on top of the prince, his mind swarming like a hive of angry bees. He opened his mouth, calling the hottest fire from the pit of his belly.

"Moreanna!" Whelin shouted.

Tavin, coming to himself in a blaze of anger and remorse, pressed the silver dagger against Whelin's throat.

"How do you know her name?" he said. "I never told you that. I never told anyone her name."

"She's screaming," a small trickle of blood seeped past the blade. Whelin's black eyes grew large. "She's screaming. She's dying. Tavin — it's you."

"Liar! Someone told you."

Prince Whelin's breath labored in his chest.

"No one else knows — about your connection. You never told."

"Then how do you know?"

The prince turned his wrist over, revealing the scar left there by the cut of the silver knife.

Tavin's grip turned white. He dragged the tip of the dagger beneath Whelin's rib cage. His vision blurred.

"We share more than blood," Whelin said. "I can hear her now as you once did."

Tavin's hand trembled.

"You used to see with the same eyes," Whelin continued. "You used to be as close as one person in two bodies. It changed when your mother died. After your father left, you pushed her even further away. She tried to find you again, but you blocked everything but the coldest thoughts. She needs you, Tavin. And instead of healing, you're sending her nothing but the poison and darkness."

"Why would she tell you all this and not me?"

"She had no choice," Whelin said. "You stopped listening, Tavin. It's been you all along. You're killing her."

Tavin dropped the dagger as if burnt. Fire lit his eyes and died. He rolled off Whelin and crumpled to the ground.

"Tavin …" Whelin reached out a hand. It shook as it dropped

onto Tavin shoulder, but Whelin's eyes revealed only pity.

Tavin screamed, throwing his rage up at the starry sky. It was true; he hated his father for leaving him when he needed him most. He hated his mother for dying. But most of all he hated himself for not being able to save either of them. He'd failed them all — and now his failure was killing Moreanna.

"You are right," Whelin said wearily. "We are in a war." Whelin looked pale, but his hand grew steady again. His throat healed before Tavin's eyes. He pressed his palm over Tavin's heart, against his scar. "It begins in here."

Tavin rubbed his face and looked away. He was quiet for a long time, trying to process his thoughts. When he finally spoke , he was unable to meet the prince in the eye.

"I think I could use a cup of coffee," he said.

Tavin shook as he poured coffee for himself and herbal tea for Whelin. Moreanna called the way he made coffee a 'Boy Scout': a quarter cream, a quarter coffee, and half sugar. She could be such a brat.

Across from him, crowded between Oma's small round table and the wall, Whelin sipped his tea.

"You didn't look scared," said Tavin. "How did you know I wouldn't kill you?"

"I didn't," answered Whelin.

Tavin slumped back in his chair. He let out a slow breath, running his fingers nervously through his hair.

"Don't you ever panic and screw up?"

The prince turned his head to look out the window. "I'm not afraid to die, if that's what you mean."

"I — I guess I can tell what she sees in you," Tavin said. "Aria told me about you guys getting married, right before Opa — " Tavin broke off. It would be some time before he could talk about the last moments of his grandfather's life.

"It was my father's idea," Whelin said slowly. "It will help bring much stability to her kingdom. We have a … gentler view of many things. If Aria and I are one, my family may be able to influence her people for good."

Tavin took a gulp of his coffee. "And you love her." He didn't mean it as a question.

Prince Whelin walked to the window. "She is young," he said. "She needs time to mature, to grow into the quiet grace of womanhood. She will be a dutiful companion."

Tavin choked, snorting coffee. He coughed, trying to clear his nasal passages. Luckily the prince's back was turned. "You guys are going to get along great," Tavin said, a small seed of hope blossoming in his chest. "I can tell."

Whelin nodded distractedly. He pulled up the window latch and slid the glass wide open.

"Can you smell it?" he asked.

Tavin shivered as the night air rushed into Oma's warm little kitchen. He sniffed. The breeze was dry and it carried with it the sour smell of ash.

"I smelt it back in the fields," replied Tavin. "I figured it was because of the explosion."

Whelin shook his head. His gaze looked as if it could cut glass.

"It's more than that. Etheria is burning."

Tavin stood so quickly he knocked his chair over. In his mind, he saw Demetre. His voice, a voice like rocks in the desert, had told him to let them burn.

Now he knew what it meant. "How is that possible?" he asked.

"The Unmaker. He has crossed over and is trying to return to his former strength; I believe he is very close."

"What happened?" Tavin felt cold. The hair on his arms stood up.

"In order to return as he was, the Unmaker needs a place of powerful magic to draw from. He has returned to the place of his creation, the Pool of Chaos. There he gathers his strength. Now he exists only as a shadow, but the power of the pool may soon change that."

"Why aren't you fighting?" Tavin could hear the dull horror behind Whelin's words. A suspicion built in his mind, one that he dared not face unless he knew for sure.

"The Unmaker is guarded by an Elemental," Whelin said. "They are possibly the strongest clan in Etheria. They often sleep for centuries in the high places of our world but when they choose to act, there are few powerful enough to oppose them."

"Several hours ago," Whelin continued, "an Elemental landed near the pool in his Fire element. Everything he touches turns to fire and ash. The attack was so swift that it took us awhile before we even realized what happened. The mages of Etheria have gathered, but at their best, they are doing little better than containing the fires. I came here to talk with you but also to plead with your grandfather. There is only one type of mage that can rival the power of an Elemental."

Tavin's coffee had gone cold. He dumped the leftovers down the sink. His mouth felt dry. "Opa said there were others."

"None close enough," replied Whelin.

Tavin licked his lips. "You do know I've only had my powers one night, right? It takes months to train."

Whelin managed a tight smile. "You learn quickly."

Tavin couldn't meet Whelin's eyes. "Didn't you tell me not to go back? Didn't you say something about dying?"

"Tavin, you are a Guardian. You have fought it but it remains in your blood. Every fiber of your being fights to protect the weak. Only a Guardian would have the courage to fight monsters like the Chill or stand up to the Fairy King."

"But they hate me," Tavin said.

"Their hearts have been turned to the dark Queen; the ones that hurt you are not what they were meant to be. They need someone to show them a different path."

Tavin wrung a tea towel through his hands. He could hear the ticking clock count off the long seconds of silence as he struggled.

"Tavin," Whelin spoke quietly. "Perhaps this is a way for you to fight the darkness that eats at your soul."

Tavin remained frozen to the spot. Whelin's words dug into his chest, bringing him both fear and hope. Could he really die for someone that hated him?

"Not for you," he said, almost too quietly to hear. He cleared his throat and tried again. "I'll fight, but not for you." He hesitated. "Opa loved your world even though it cost his life, and Moreanna trusted you enough to send you her thoughts. I'll do it for them. And maybe you're right." He swallowed. "Maybe I can fix some of the damage I've done to Moreanna. But I have one condition."

Whelin looked grave, yet a light in his eyes betrayed a smile. "What is it?"

Tavin coughed roughly. "Whatever happens, you take care of my sister. If things go bad, I want to die knowing she'll be okay."

Whelin nodded. "Consider it done, little brother."

"Its Foe Draws Near..."

I wish I could hear you, Morry.

The wind buffeted his eardrums like music at a rock concert. The air became hot and dry. The smell of smoke was sharp and acrid, stinging Tavin's eyes. He plummeted several feet before thrusting his wings open with a snap.

Now I know why my head hurts all the time. You were trying to get close and I just pushed back.

Tavin looked around to gain his bearings, but the smoke was too thick. He glanced to his left. Whelin, wearing wings that looked like two bursts of flame from his back, shouted something and dropped into a spinning dive. Tavin followed his lead. Tears rolled from his eyes as he dove. His lungs felt as if they were on fire.

You look just like mom, you know that? You act just like her, too, always worrying over me. Sometimes it's hard to be around you, you bring back all these memories …It made it worse when dad left.

Tavin spotted a bright flash of green. They dropped lower and the smoke abruptly cleared. Tavin thankfully gulped clean air, hardly noticing the thick-leaved trees.

I'm ready to listen now. I'm ready to change, even if things go badly. I'm going to do something you can really be proud of — I'm going to give you a memory to hold for the rest of your life.

Someone shouted a warning. Tavin blinked with surprise then smashed into the ground, leaving a dark skid mark through layers of wet moss. He dug his heels down then slammed into something rubbery, bounced back several feet, and landed in a bush. Tavin rubbed his eyes in bewilderment, happily unhurt.

"Okay … it's official. Your landings suck."

Aria stood where Tavin's skid mark began, her arms crossed. Beside her, Prince Whelin toed gracefully out of the air like a ballet dancer.

Aria stalked towards Tavin. Her dark hair was in knots and her skin smudged with ash. Her clothing was torn and dirty. Two steel swords hung from her hips. She looked like she'd been through a war.

Her mood wasn't much better.

"What is he doing here?"

Whelin pulled her protectively to his side, but for whose protection Tavin wasn't sure. "It was for the best."

She snarled. "If he's the best, then we're doomed."

"Opa's dead," Tavin said. He fought hard to keep the accusation from his voice but it still leaked through.

That shut her up.

Whelin cleared his throat. "Did you get it?" he asked Aria.

"Get what?" Tavin shook his head trying to get the clumps of mud and twigs out of his hair.

Aria flushed. "I've found out where it is."

Whelin turned towards Tavin. "She means the black sword," he explained. "Without it we can't get through the barrier that the other mages have set up to contain the Elemental. The barrier only gets stronger if we use any magic on it."

Just the thought of the sword made Tavin's heart speed up. "What does it do?" he asked.

"It has a simple but significant power," Whelin said. "It can cut through anything. What did you discover, Aria?"

Tavin felt his heart sink. Somehow, he already knew the answer. Aria had that crazy look in her eye.

"Madame Caveat has it," she said, "and she's not alone."

The trees hung top-heavy above them, bowed by thick, rubbery leaves. A carpet of slimy weeds disguised deep sinkholes and hid small, sharp-toothed animals. Aria and Tavin flew low, batting at insects. Below, Whelin ran as swiftly as a silver dart, streaking across the top of the swamp weeds, his coat gleaming in the grey light.

Tavin looked sidelong at Aria, watching as she bobbed over and under branches. He sped ahead of her and turned sharply, forcing her to snap open her wings and jerk to a halt. She shoved at his chest with both hands, her pale cheeks flushed with two spots of anger.

"Stay out of my way," she said.

Tavin shook his head, squaring himself off in front of her. "Look," he said. "I was a jerk. I'm sorry."

Aria frowned. "You're apologizing?" she asked.

"When I saw my grandfather … well, anyways, I don't blame you. It wasn't your fault."

She crossed her arms. "What do you want?"

Tavin shrugged. "Nothing. Things have changed since the last time you saw me. I'm different now. I'm stronger."

Tavin snapped his fingers, willing a small flame to blossom into being. Tavin watched Aria's shocked expression with a crooked smile. "You see? I can take care of myself."

Aria looked at him over the ball of flame, her expression stunned.

"Oh, and … It's not going to work out with Whelin," Tavin shrugged. "I'm sorry for that as well."

Aria flushed purple. "It's none of your business," she snarled.

Tavin held out his hands. "I'm not looking for a fight okay? I'd just like to be friends again."

"Then why'd you say it?"

Tavin smiled. "It's just this sense that I have."

Tavin sped up and flew ahead of her, skimming over the treetops. Let her mull over that one, he thought with satisfaction. I can wait.

The air smelt burnt, the wind was cold, and there was little sun. Aria pointed down to a break in the trees. They dropped down again, landing on the shore of a flat, gray lake.

The sky was lost beyond a low ceiling of fog. Long fingers of mist curled out over the greenish water.

Whelin snorted, shaking his ebony antlers. "This place has a bad smell," he said.

Something crunched beneath Tavin's foot. He'd stepped on a tiny skull. It looked human but was hardly bigger than the palm of his hand.

"Scaredy cat," Aria mocked his expression before looking out over the water. "The sword is on an island in the middle of this lake."

It feels like a trap, thought Tavin. *I could probably use some of your brains about now, Morry.*

Whelin tossed his head and waded into the green water. Tavin watched him go in surprise. "He never hesitates, does he?" Tavin asked.

Aria shook her head and ventured a small smile. "Race you there." She vibrated her wings and jumped back into the air. Tavin followed, forming a ball of fire, his eyes straining to see through the mist.

At first, the lake appeared endless. Aria soon fell back to fly closer to Tavin and his small fireball. Vapor soaked their clothing through. Unseen creatures chattered and howled at them through the mist. Finally, Tavin caught his first glimpse of the island as a dark smudge through the fog. It grew solid and bold, a hulking mammoth of sharp, splintered rock. Dried grass and dead trees clung to its sides, reminding Tavin of dead spiders on a windowsill.

Whelin swam tirelessly below, his gazed fixed upon their goal.

They landed upon a shore of clattering black pebbles. Whelin dragged free of the water, shaking muck from his white flanks. Aria freed her blades, the dull steel glinting ominously.

A small mountain, wreathed by mist, dug its roots into the beach. A faint trail, like a wisp of grey smoke, curled up its face.

Aria pointed towards the path. "We're on their territory now," she said. "It's probably best to follow the path and stay low as we can. The monsters that live here spend most of their time in the air."

Tavin, determined to go first, set his feet and hands upon the steep mountain trail. Water slicked the rocks making the footing treacherous, and the craggy rock face bit into his palms. The path was less of a trail and more of a near-vertical scramble. Tavin climbed steadily, stepping around crumbling ledges and splintered handholds.

The island rolled open below him: a wide flat plain crisscrossed by deep crevices. Thick fog crowded against the rocky shores, shrouding the swamp from sight.

Tavin reached the top, his palms red, his legs shaky. Whelin appeared shortly afterward. He'd climbed in his human form, lithe as a mountain goat. Aria took a while longer, summiting with dark looks and panting heavily.

They stood at the base of a low round hill. A gigantic white tree, with long gnarly roots, clawed at the crown. The ends of the tree's branches jabbed at the sky like blackened fire pokers. Mist ran in rivulets down its wide, dead trunk.

A dripping, wagon-wheel web wove its way through the branches of the tree. In the heart of the web, less than a hundred feet from where they stood, hung the black sword, buried in a leather scabbard.

Tavin's heart slowed. A black creature, with dark feathered wings wrapped about its head and body, perched upon a thick branch near the sword. Sharp talons, as long as pencils, gripped it to the branch.

Aria eased silently into place beside Tavin.

"Is it asleep?" Tavin whispered.

Aria looked troubled. "They never sleep, never fully," she replied.

Tavin noticed a curious shape drifting down from the sky. He reached out and caught it. It was a long black feather, the end tipped with red.

A long shriek cut like a whip through the gloom. An answering cry rang out from another direction, echoing with laughter.

"What are they?" Tavin spun in a tight circle, trying to get a glimpse of the monsters.

"Harpies," Aria turned, instinctively pressing her back against his. She pushed her dark hair back from her forehead and raised a sword. "They're from the Chill clan, sisters to Caveat. They also drink blood."

Tavin saw the shape of a black wing flitter through the mist; he felt the rush of wind upon his face.

"Steady," Whelin bounced lightly upon the balls of his feet, his dagger in his hand. "Here they come!"

Aria screamed.

The creatures erupted out of the fog on giant black wings with their arms outstretched. The monsters were naked; their skin hung from their bodies in molting grayish lumps and their long seaweed hair was the color of swamp water.

Tavin flung a fireball. It exploded with a flash of light. The harpies shrieked in fury. Several of the creatures climbed above their heads, slashing at their faces with long talons.

"Good move, Tavin … duck!" Aria swept a sword on a flashing circle above their heads. Whelin flowed around them in a blur of shape-shifting light, striking at the harpies with both dagger and hooves. "Tavin," he cried, "Get the sword!"

Whelin and Aria moved fast, their blades sharp and accurate, slicing into any monster that dared come close. As a group, they climbed the hill. Seeing an opening, Tavin left his friends and darted the last few feet to the tree. He climbed quickly up its sloping trunk, ducking through the sticky strands of webbing. The giant harpy above him remained perfectly still.

Tavin could already feel the weight of the sword in his hand. He lay on his belly and wormed forward along a thick branch, hardly daring to breathe as he drew closer to his prize. He reached out and touched its hilt.

With a slow angry hiss and the scrape of tree bark, the harpy awoke. Her head emerged above the black wings with hair black as oil and a face made of rolling folds of flesh. A large slit in the harpy's forehead revealed a single red eye.

A mouth, wide as a cave, opened and released a long keening wail.

The noise slammed into Tavin's mind and he flew backwards. He landed on the ground, clutching his head in pain. He gasped and threw a fireball towards the monster. The flame was weak but the giant harpy broke her cry with a hiss. Tavin dragged himself to his feet. The harpy opened her wings and fell towards Tavin in vengeful rage. Tavin shoved outwards with his hands and a wave of fire enveloped her, turning her wings to flame. The harpy gave another keening wail and shot into the sky, slipping away into the mist.

For a moment, Tavin couldn't move, deafened by the harpy's parting scream. Then he saw Aria. She'd fallen to her knees. A thin trickle of purple blood ran out her ear.

Tavin pulled himself to Aria's side. He'd almost reached her when a black shape dived at him over the hill. The giant red-eyed harpy hooked her talons into Tavin's cheek and dragged him down the hill towards the cliff. Tavin yelled and tore free. Both Whelin and Aria lay stunned upon the ground. Tavin rolled onto his back and crossed his arms, throwing a shield of fire about him.

The harpy fell to the ground, her wings charred and heavy with blood. Tavin kicked at her and she grabbed his ankle, pulling him further towards the edge of the cliff. Tavin tried to fly back but the harpy weighed him down.

"Come, little one," she said. "Come with me and rest from your weary labors."

She spread her wings and rose from the ground, still grasping his ankle.

Tavin gaped. Her voice was thick and sweet as honey. It flowed over him like molasses. Time slowed. The harpy changed. She became the most beautiful woman Tavin had ever seen. Her dark hair cascaded down her body like ink. Her wings were angel wings. She smiled so serenely that Tavin was unable to believe she could lie. He relaxed. The harpy pulled on his ankle, drawing him close to her.

Suddenly she shrieked in pain. The spell shattered and Aria yanked a steel sword from the harpy's side. The harpy cursed and spat at Aria, releasing Tavin. Aria sliced the sword across the harpy's throat.

"Witch," she said. She kicked the monster over the side of the cliff. Aria wiped her sword on her sleeve and looked at Tavin with a crooked smile. "Looks like you still need taking care of after all."

Tavin stared at her in pure awe. "I'm so in love with you," he said.

Aria frowned. "What did you say?"

"Nothing." Tavin grinned and climbed to his feet. Aria smiled back in confusion and turned towards the tree.

A rush of wind blew Tavin back. Two harpies snatched Aria's arms and dragged her into the air. Tavin yelled and ran forward. A hand yanked him back.

"The sword, Tavin!" Whelin cried. "You must get it. I'll help Aria!" The prince ran towards the path and leapt down with the poise and swiftness of a mountain cat.

Tavin looked over his shoulder. The other harpies turned their backs on him, eager to play with their new catch. Tavin singed their wings with fireballs. Far below, Whelin leapt from the mountain and onto the wide plain. Aria freed one of her arms and hacked viciously at her attackers. Tavin ran forward. There was no way he was going to listen to a snotty prince and abandon Aria. His eyes brightened with fire, his wings hummed. He leapt into the air. Then something snagged his jacket, throwing him down onto the rocky ground.

Madame Caveat sidled out from behind the large tree with a venomous smile. Her long spider legs unfolded like a flower in the sun and pulled upon the cord that she'd used to snare Tavin.

"What's the matter, pretty pretty?" Madame Caveat said. "Your friend's in danger?"

From the distance, there was a scream of rage. Tavin looked in time to see a harpy rip Aria's wings from her back. Whelin saw it too, running forward in a streak of silver. Tavin paled as Aria plummeted towards the rocks, holding his breath. Whelin dashed beneath Aria and broke her fall, catching her small body in his arms.

Tavin said a prayer of thanks and turned back to Caveat. He growled low in his throat. "Leave them alone."

Madame Caveat sneered, clacking her black teeth. Tavin drew a deep breath, feeling fire gather in his belly. Madame Caveat bunched her fat body and sprung forward, slicing a poison tipped claw down through the air and stopping it an inch away from the side of his neck. Tavin's hands flared with fire.

"Spit webbing at me and you'll go up in flames, poison or no," he said.

Madame Caveat hesitated, her poison-tipped claws hovering. "No matter," she replied. "He says not to kill you. He says he likes you."

"Who?"

Madame Caveat's small black eyes glimmered with malice. "*Him*," she said. "He gives his greetings and also a message."

"What?" Tavin drew in a slow breath.

"Go home. Leave. Use your new power to protect your own world." Madame Caveat's shawls fluttered around her misshapen form. "He will see that your family is safe from more attacks — forever. He is also wise. He can teach you many things." She leered. "Make a better world for you."

On the rocky plain below, there was a cry. Tavin looked over his shoulder and saw Whelin running for cover, carrying Aria. The monsters sped after them, screeching riotously, their talons reaching for soft flesh. Beneath his shirt, Tavin's scar began glowing with brilliant light. He clenched his fists.

Madame Caveat scurried back and cocked her head, her expression calculating. She seemed as if she were waiting for something.

Whelin transformed into a stag in a flash of white light. He found shelter beside a boulder, and pinned Aria between the rock and his mighty bulk, shielding her from attack. The monsters shrieked with delight. Swooping in, they tore deep gouges in the prince's white flanks and shoulders. Silver blood streamed freely from his wounds, slicking the ground beneath him, but he refused to move and expose Aria.

Tavin turned back towards Madame Caveat, the world coming sharply into focus.

He felt the power build within him.

"Stay and your family dies," hissed Caveat. "And all your kind. He does not forget."

"No," Tavin answered. "We will fight." Tavin jumped forward and locked his arms around Madame Caveat's waist. He felt the fire rush through his limbs. She cried out in rage and blindly slashed at him with her poisoned talons. Her many tattered shawls alight, Madame Caveat flared up like a roman candle.

She howled and struggled to get free. Tavin only tightened his grip. The fire burned even hotter. Finally, Tavin let go and stumbled backwards, not a hair singed. He gaped at Caveat in stunned horror, gagging on the smell of burning flesh.

Seconds later, it was over. The fire died leaving nothing but a blackened corpse, burned beyond recognition.

The harpies grew quiet. They stopped their attack and watched him with hard black gazes. Tavin glared back and built a large fireball. Several of the leaders screamed a warning and shot away into the mist; the others quickly followed.

Tavin looked down from the top of the hill and met Whelin's eyes. The prince nodded wearily, moving away from the rock to allow a tearful Aria to scramble free.

Numbly, Tavin climbed the white tree and pulled the sword free. It slid easily into his hands. Tavin welcomed it back, feeling his heart swell with the sense of its presence. The sword was his; it always had been. He tied the scabbard about his waist.

He missed seeing the small black spider climb out from under Madame Caveat's corpse and slip out of sight down a crevice.

Tavin paused at the edge of the mountain. A fireball, no bigger than the size of an orange, formed at the ends of his fingertips. Tavin played with it for a moment, changing the shape and size with a simple act of will. His right hand rested comfortably upon the hilt of the black blade. He inhaled sharply, a forbidding shiver moving down his spine.

Moreanna, he thought, *I've done some things you won't believe.*

"*Through Chaos, By Fire...*"

Whelin carried Aria across the lake and through the swamp, while Tavin flew ahead and scouted for trouble. Looking back at them, Tavin couldn't help but notice that Whelin's deep wounds had not healed and that he struggled to keep pace. Aria held a naked sword ready at her side, and often leaned over to hug Whelin's neck in a fearful embrace.

The air grew thick with smoke and yellow sulfur. Below him, the rubbery trees of the swamp ended abruptly. Tavin's throat tightened.

Charred stumps and blasted rock made it feel as if they'd stumbled on a bombsite. The ground dropped away and Whelin stopped on the edge of a low precipice. Aria scrambled from his back, a look of stunned horror on her face. Tavin landed carefully beside her.

The destruction before them was a perfect circle, about a mile in diameter. Tall burning stumps, splintered at their blackened tops, were all that remained of the forest. The earth was a ragged open wound, oozing black, boiling mud and smoking tar. Large stones, whitened by the immense heat, lay strewn about like bleached bones. The sky rolled with dark clouds like a boiling pot.

A large clear dome of flickering magic sealed away the destruction, for the moment containing the fire that raged within, and protecting them from the full force of the heat. The mage shield flickered with streaks of rainbow-colored light like shooting stars across its surface.

Tavin's forehead beaded with sweat. The shimmering heat caused the landscape to blur before his eyes and sapped his resolve. Aria swallowed nervously, and even Whelin seemed paler than usual.

"The shield is already weakening." Aria watched the colored mage lights flare brightly then fade away.

"What's that?" Tavin's eyes caught a flash of green and blue near the center of the crater. The bit of color upon the burning landscape glimmered like a tiny polished jewel.

"That is the Pool of Chaos," Whelin turned, his sides stained by the bloody wounds that still struggled to heal. "I should probably tell you, it is forbidden for humans to go near the pool."

Tavin laughed; he couldn't help it. Bubbly hysteria gripped him for a moment. Tears came to his eyes and he wiped them away. He hiccupped, trying to regain control of his emotions. Aria made a face.

"What's so funny?"

Despite the great heat, Tavin buttoned the jacket Opa'd given to him tightly closed. He unfolded his wings and flapped them a few times, trying to look more in control than he felt.

"Nothing," he said. "I just seem to be born for breaking rules."

Tavin slid the black sword from its sheath and pressed the tip of the sword to the mage barrier. Immediately the magical wall began to crackle and send out rainbow colored sparks. He swung around, startling Aria who was half a step behind him.

"Hey."

"Hey." Aria sounded tired.

Tavin wanted to grab her and fly somewhere far away, somewhere where it would be just them — no princes, no wars — just them and the wild flowers on a warm summer day. Instead, he smiled and planted a light kiss on her forehead. "It's going to be okay."

Tavin lifted his sword and plunged it deep into the barrier over his head. A powerful wind roared through the rift and beams of energy arched out from the breech. Tavin leaned into the wind and dragged his sword downward. The edges of the tear blackened and curled back. Soon it was big enough.

He squeezed his eyes shut and jumped through.

As he passed through, Tavin opened his hand and sent a ball of fire into the shield behind him. Strengthened by Tavin's magic, the barrier rippled and sealed tightly shut, cutting off the startled cries of his companions. He didn't look back. He felt his new power welling up inside of him. The feeling was both frightening and intoxicating.

Ever since the island, Tavin had known he had to face the Elemental alone. Whelin was hurt worse than he would admit, and even if Aria still had her wings, she would stand no chance against a monster that destroyed worlds.

"*Moreanna,*" he whispered. He shut his eyes and sent a message of love to his sister. He opened his heart to her, sharing the pain he'd kept locked inside. He opened himself and let light shine into the darkness. Perhaps he had some ways to go before he could forgive his father, his mother, and himself, but now at least he was ready to begin.

Tavin clenched the sword in his right hand and clumsily jumped into the air. His wings labored to carry him into the hot currents. Soon he was just high enough to pass across the spiting mud and sinister boiling tar.

Through the shimmering waves of heat, Tavin easily spotted the bright green patch of land amidst the blasted destruction. He began sweating freely. His clothing beneath his jacket was drenched. The boiling mud spat burning chunks of dirt into the air. Heated stones hissed like angry snakes and sent up waves of heat.

Tavin struggled higher, his eyes fixed upon his goal. The patch of green earth looked like an island of paradise in the middle of hell. He pressed forward, feeling resistance in the air as he neared the green oasis. He forced his way forward and the air became cool. Tavin landed gingerly upon the short green grass. The blasted world behind him seemed impossible next to the calm beauty around him. A little ways away there stood a thicket of smooth skinned trees.

Tavin opened a hand and willed a ball of flame to come. His magical fire flared into existence, brighter and hotter than he'd expected. Tavin frowned, quieting the flame and bringing it under control. He tossed it towards the trees, but nothing happened. The fire simply died out, leaving the landscape unharmed.

He was no expert, but even he could sense the magic in the air. As he drew close to the tangled thicket, he had a sudden inspiration and passed his hand over the branches as if he were opening a Gate.

His hunch proved to be correct. The tree branches parted, forming a small winding path down a grassy slope.

Past the trees, a perfectly round pool sat in the center of a hidden dell. The water was as smooth as glass, yet beneath its surface bright pearly colors swirled together in mesmerizing patterns.

Wrapped in a fiery circle about the pool was the Elemental.

The creature looked like a cross between a dragon and a lion. It had a flat snout, long whiskers, and a thick mane running down its back. The Elemental's body was bright red, long, sinewy, and scaled. It rested upon heavily muscled legs with long hooked claws. Despite the magical coolness of the pool, the heat emanating from the creature was nearly unbearable. Around his neck, the fire Elemental wore an ornate jade necklace with a fire symbol etched into the center. Tavin, partially shielded behind a tree, had trouble looking directly at it.

"Tavin." A whisper moved through the trees like wind. Tavin turned in a circle trying to guess its source.

"Tavin, I knew you'd come."

A chill ran through Tavin. Instantly he remembered the creepy feeling he'd felt back in the swamp.

"You followed me," he said. "You've been watching."

Tavin located the speaker. He stood within the coils of the Elemental, next to the Pool of Chaos. Bright misty colors flowed up from the pool and into his skin. He seemed frail, like a porcelain doll, and remained slightly transparent. Seeing Tavin move towards him, he stood and tugged the pale gloves he wore neatly into place and straightened his velvet jacket so it hung perfectly across his slim shoulders. His small eyes glowed like two little hot coals.

"Demetre." Tavin said it with acceptance; he wondered how long he'd known. "You're the Unmaker."

Demetre cocked his head to one side as if he didn't quite understand Tavin's words. Then he smiled sleepily. "What a nasty name, but I guess they would see it that way. I only tried to rid the world of pain. We were made broken, Tavin. The only way to fix things is to start over again. You understand."

"But you're a murderer."

Demetre shook his head. "I don't kill; I take things out of existence. Isn't there anything you wish never happened? Or a person you wish just didn't exist?"

Tavin didn't have anything to say. He'd wished those very things countless times.

"The others betrayed me," Demetre continued. "They couldn't see I was trying to make things better. But I've come back. This pool birthed me and it will do so again."

Tavin freed his sword.

"I came to stop you, Demetre."

Demetre laughed. "Who gave you your new powers? If you let them, the others will try to hold you back, to cage you the way they caged me. But I'm offering you freedom Tavin: freedom to be everything you ever wanted and dreamed. When this world is cleansed and remade, you'll thank me. They all will."

Tavin felt a stab of pain in his stomach. Could Demetre be right? The Shadowlands was a dying world, eating itself from the inside out with hatred and suspicion. Murderers walked boldly and the few who fought for good seemed doomed to suffer. Most did not even deserve to live. Was it time to wipe the slate clean?

Demetre saw his hesitation. "Imagine it, Tavin: a strong, healthy, living world. No more sickness, disease, or pain. No more ugly weakness."

Tavin. Moreanna's voice came to him, sweet and stronger than it had been in years.

Moreanna. Hope rose in Tavin's heart. He shook his head, clearing out the cobwebs.

"I've got this rat," he said. "He's a greedy scavenger and messy. He's also ugly. He'd probably be the first thing to go in your world. But he doesn't deserve to be unmade."

Demetre scoffed. "A rat? Who cares about a rat?"

Realization, like a ray of sunshine, beamed onto Tavin's mind. "I do," he said. "I love him, and love makes ugly things beautiful. No one's going to touch my rat, or my friends, or my family, or even all the messed up people I don't know yet. We can all be better."

Demetre snorted. "Hope makes me laugh."

Tavin, Moreanna said. *Kick his butt.*

Tavin raised his sword. "Sorry. Maybe you were a friend to me, so I'm sorry to do this. But you can't have this world."

Demetre's boyish face grew hard. He lifted a delicate hand and pointed towards Tavin. The Elemental, who had remained as stone while they talked, raised its gigantic head.

"Kill him."

The Elemental looked at Tavin with eyes like molten lava; it climbed ponderously to its feet.

"How I burn." The Elemental spoke in a voice as ancient as the mountains with the rumbling power of thunder. "I have tasted the water of a thousand rivers; flown across a hundred seas. The blood of my victims cries from the ground, yet my thirst is not slaked."

The Elemental's voice deepened and grew louder at the same time. Each carefully spoken word caused a tremor in the earth.

"I have lain upon the ice beds in the north. I have swum the depths of the sea. I have sought the beating heart of Earth and touched the darkness of space. There was no rest for me there."

The creature slowly raised itself from the ground. Each scale glistened like a hot coal. "This blessed pool called to me. I have answered and laid my burden to rest."

Tavin's eyes streamed with stinging tears. The heat struck him like a wall. The Elemental took a step towards him and the earth shook so violently that Tavin fell against the tree, clutching it for support.

"But now I have been awakened! I burn and I writhe! I obey!" roared the Elemental.

Huge wings of living flame sprouted from the Elemental's back and opened in a whirlwind of fire, spreading across the magical clearing. The dragon beat them slowly, stirring up a scorching wind as he rose into the air. There was a hissing rumble, and Tavin scrambled for cover as a stream of fire blasted past him.

Tavin opened his small orange-colored wings. He summoned a white ball of fire and pulled the sword free. He gripped it tightly in his hand as if drawing strength from the blade.

"I'm a Guardian," he whispered to himself, drawing on the memory of Opa and the strength he found there. "I was given magic to protect this world."

Tavin climbed into the sky with a battle yell, his wings beating at the hot air. His skin tingled and his mind felt sharp. For the first time in a long time, he could think clearly. The Elemental looked down in rage. He dropped his jaw and breathed a river of fire, forcing Tavin to turn and dive quickly.

Tavin felt a change in air pressure and rolled into an updraft. He shot above the Elemental. The dragon roared and spewed more fire.

Tavin threw up his arms and a burst of magical flame shot from his fists. Red lava erupted as the two flames met, dropping a liquid stream of fire into the bubbling mud pools below.

The Elemental sped towards Tavin like a train. Its lion mouth gaped wide, and its huge wings beat the air like a thunderstorm.

Tavin closed his wings and rolled to the side, clipping his shoulder on a claw as the beast lunged forward. He swung the black sword downwards and through the fire, wounding his enemy.

Great drops of steaming blood fell hissing from the Elemental's forearm. Tavin shouted and pressed his hands together. A fireball, larger than a man, hurtled towards the Elemental. The beast absorbed the attack with a roar and spat back molten rock.

Tavin had no time to defend. Heat washed over him and through him, and then was gone. He gasped with surprise. He was unharmed.

The Elemental leapt forward, flashing teeth and deadly claws. Tavin tumbled over backwards, falling out of control as he tried to get out of the way. He dodged beneath the Elemental, slashing upward at its underbelly. His sword whistled cleanly through the air, then shuddered to a halt.

Tavin saw a flash of green. He'd caught his blade in the jade necklace about the Elemental's throat. The sword that could cut through anything was stuck. The Elemental shook violently and dropped into a spinning dive. Tavin held on, gripping the black sword with both hands and pressing down into the jade.

With a crack like a cannon shot, the necklace exploded. Flying shards of jade whipped past Tavin slicing through his jacket, arms and chest. He was hurtled backwards.

He was falling. He'd lost his sword. His fluttering attempts to slow himself threw him into a dizzying corkscrew. Wind roared past his ears; the ground spun in patterns of gray and brown.

Tavin began to black out.

The last thing he remembered was the strong smell of freshly turned earth, a deep voice like distant thunder, and falling rain.

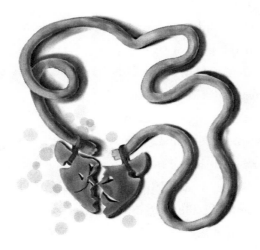

Falling Rain

White and silver-lined clouds streaked the sky. Tavin felt soft rain on his face. He lay on something solid. Tavin put his hands out and pushed himself up. A glassy clear surface suspended him in the air. Rainbow colors flashed beneath his fingers. He dipped towards earth then rose again steadily. A gentle wind fanned his face. On either side of him, gigantic crystal wings flashed with the color of the sunrise.

"I thought you'd like the view," a deep gentle voice, wild as roses, spoke to Tavin.

Tavin ran his fingers over the surface below him, catching the edges in the glass with his fingernail. A small piece came off and Tavin used his fingers to find the shape. "It's a scale," he said. His mind whirled with questions.

The creature laughed. "You may keep it."

"You're the Elemental," Tavin held the scale up in wonder, watching it sparkle in the sun. "You caught me."

"We are slaves to jade," the Elemental said. "When you broke the necklace, you broke the enchantment that bound me to fire and to agony. I am called Jin."

Tavin looked down. They flew in a wide circle around the swamp. The rain continued to fall, each drop polished to a rainbow shine. Tavin saw the crater like a ragged scar torn in the earth. As he looked, it seemed as if the dark mud lightened in color, taking on a fresh green hue.

"It was the Unmaker who did this," Jin said. "He bound me so that I would be driven mad and seek solace at the pool. With me there, he believed that none could approach. He would be free to harness the pool's power and fully awaken from the world of dreams."

Tavin gazed at the world below him. They flew higher than he'd ever dared. Dim stars peaked through a break in the clouds. They seemed close enough to catch with his hands.

"We have to go back," said Tavin. "We have to stop him."

Jin shook his head. "He is already gone. He fled the moment his enchantment on me broke. He knows he cannot stand against the combined magic of an unbound Elemental and a true Guardian. But make no mistake, he will try again." Jin's voice grew softer. "You bear his touch, little one, as I now do. I can feel it. Your power is not entirely your own. You must take care."

Fear pressed against Tavin's mind. "It's true," he said. "I let him get into my mind. I don't know what's worse. That he tried to use me, or that I almost understand why he did."

"You do not need to fear," Jin replied. "You fought for love; you were willing to die for it. This is a quality that the Unmaker does not possess."

Tavin looked down. Far below, upon the edge of the crater, a small group had gathered: goblins, fairies, Elche, and many more creatures he did not recognize. They were all looking up at him.

"Do you think this changes things?" Tavin asked.

Jin laughed with a low rumble deep in his belly. "It is a start. You have made some loyal friends today. Don't underestimate their value."

Tavin caught a glimmer of white. Standing a little apart from the crowd was Whelin. Blood and dirt washed from the prince's sides in cleansing rivers. Aria sat again upon his back.

She looked up at Tavin, watching his triumphant flight. Even from a distance, Tavin thought he could see a smile on her lips.

"*The Unmaker Is Coming*"

$\mathcal{A}$ trail of torn clothing and slimy mud once again traced a path between Tavin's bedroom and the washroom around the corner. After a long shower and a much-needed rest, Tavin lay on his bed, lost in thought.

He held the Elemental's smooth scale in his hand, his fingers worrying about its blunt edges. Sensing the gentle brush of his sister's presence across his thoughts, he opened his eyes.

She stood with a smile at the side of his bed, dressed in black skirts and a high-collared jacket. *You did it*, she said. *I'm strong again.*

Tavin shook his head, tears coming to his eyes. *It was me all along*, he replied. *I hated the world for taking mom away and I hated dad for leaving. My heart was sick and it was killing you.*

Dad still loves us, Moreanna replied. *One day he'll remember it.*

I know. Tavin blew out his cheeks. *You've missed a lot, Morry. You have no idea just how crazy it's been.*

Moreanna grinned crookedly. *I can guess. I picked up a little at the end. I'll be there soon, Tavin. You can tell me everything.* She leaned over and planted a ghostly kiss upon his cheek before vanishing. *I'm proud of you, little brother.*

Tavin chewed his lip, alone again. Obviously, he wasn't the only mage in the family, but how would Moreanna react when she learned the full truth? She didn't know it, but her life was about to change forever.

Tavin ran his fingers through his hair. It was getting shaggy and it constantly fell into his eyes. It wasn't the only thing that had changed. Shallow red cuts covered his arms and three parallel gouges ran across his left cheek, nearly to his chin. They weren't deep enough to justify using the healing blood of the Elche, but they would leave a scar.

Some changes were good, he realized, and some were hard; but all of them, through love, could be made beautiful. It was what Opa had fought for: light in the darkness.

Tavin heard a door close. His head shot up. Footsteps sounded in the hall.

He yanked his covers up over his boxers. He'd forgotten to lock the door again. The footsteps hesitated outside the bathroom.

"Tavin?" Oma's voice rose sharply at the end.

To Tavin's horror, fire flared up from his hand beneath his covers. He tried to shrink the flame but it only burned hotter, causing his blanket to catch on fire. The footsteps started again. Tavin grabbed the smoldering blanket in his arms and ran towards the balcony.

A deluge of water from above stopped him cold. Tavin turned slowly around. He held the soggy and smoking comforter tightly in his arms.

Oma Nadia glared at him over the tops of her moon-shaped spectacles. Above her open palm hovered a sphere that looked like a melon-sized blue marble.

She made a quick flicking motion with her wrist and the sphere exploded over Tavin's head, drenching him a second time in cold water. Tavin spluttered with a mixture of shock and indignation. Oma's hands went to her hips.

"Once again, I see you are like an American boy," she scolded. "You sleep all day, you do no work, and when you make a mess you leave it for me to clean."

She shook her finger fiercely. "Now you are burning my nice blankets and thinking you can hide them. You have no discipline!" Oma stamped her foot. "You must train!"

Somehow, Tavin found his voice. "Train for what?" he croaked.

Oma pinned him with a menacing glare.

"To fight," she said. She paused, pursing her lips.

Her glasses flashed.

"The war has begun."

Charity Gosling currently resides with her husband Jason on Vancouver Island, BC. Her first book, Shadowlands: The Guardian, was inspired by a year spent in Germany living and working in rural villages. The sequel to this book, 'Shadowlands: The Hand of Darkness', is due to be released in February 2012.

BRIGHTER BOOKS

PUBLISHING HOUSE™

Did you love this book?

Then help us make more like it!

Rate this book on Amazon.com or your
favorite online book site,
then email us your rating / review to:

star@brighterbooks.com

*and receive an exclusive sneak-peek of one of
our upcoming books!*

Thank you for spreading the word! We are a
small press and need your support to grow!

Visit www.brighterbooks.com to continue your adventure. . .

Electric Shawn Desman
I love it Icona Pop